RESISTING HER RESCUE DOC

ALISON ROBERTS

MILLS & BOON

Published in Great Britain 2019
by Mills & Boon, an imprint of HarperCollins*Publishers*
1 London Bridge Street, London, SE1 9GF

© 2019 Alison Roberts

ISBN: 978-0-263-07971-5

MIX
Paper from
responsible sources
FSC www.fsc.org **FSC® C007454**

This book is produced from independently certified FSC™ paper
to ensure responsible forest management.
For more information visit www.harpercollins.co.uk/green.

Printed and bound in Great Britain
by CPI Group (UK) Ltd, Croydon, CR0 4YY

Alison Roberts is a New Zealander, currently lucky enough to be living in the South of France. She is also lucky enough to write for the Mills & Boon Medical Romance line. A primary school teacher in a former life, she is now a qualified paramedic. She loves to travel and dance, drink champagne, and spend time with her daughter and her friends.

Also by Alison Roberts

The Surrogate's Unexpected Miracle
Sleigh Ride with the Single Dad
The Shy Nurse's Rebel Doc
Rescued by Her Mr Right
Their Newborn Baby Gift
Twins on Her Doorstep

Rescued Hearts miniseries

The Doctor's Wife for Keeps
Twin Surprise for the Italian Doc

Discover more at millsandboon.co.uk.

CHAPTER ONE

How annoying was this?

Apart from a large motorbike that forced its way down the centre of the road, traffic on this coastal route into New Zealand's capital city, Wellington, had suddenly slowed and then come to a complete halt for no obvious reason.

Cooper Sinclair was due to meet his colleagues at the city's rescue helicopter base in just over an hour before he started his new job there tomorrow. He had, of course, planned for any contingencies that could have delayed his arrival, but that window of time had been used up by a flat tyre way back near Lake Taupo in the middle of the north island. A few minutes later, when the traffic showed no signs of beginning to move again, he followed the example of someone he could see nearer the brow of this hill, who was getting out of his car to try and find out what was going on.

'What's happening?' he called.

'Accident,' the stranger yelled back. 'Someone's driven off the road and gone down the bank just on the other side of this hill.'

The 'bank', from what Cooper could see, was more like a small cliff with a rocky beach at the bottom of the steep slope. From the top of this hill, or just over its brow, it could have been a drop of over fifteen metres and a vehicle landing on a hard surface like that from even a much smaller distance could be badly damaged with its occupants in real trouble. Turning swiftly, Cooper opened the back of his SUV to extract a small backpack. He tossed his keys to the stranger he'd been speaking to as he ran past.

'Get someone to move my car off the road if it's needed,' he said. 'I'm a paramedic. I'm going to see if I can help.'

'Good on ya, mate.' The stranger nodded. 'I'll keep an eye on your car.'

A small crowd was gathering on the side of the road and, as Cooper got closer, he could see why some people were looking so shocked. The car must have gone off the road with some speed to have buckled and then broken through the metal safety barrier like that. It had careened down the steep bank, carving a path through the undergrowth, and had come to rest, teetering on a low outcrop of rocks with waves breaking around it.

He might not be on duty but it was automatic for Cooper to go into scene assessment mode. To be looking for what extra help was going to be needed and what apparent dangers there were for any responding crews—and the public.

'Stand back,' he told people as he moved through the crowd. 'The edge of this bank doesn't look that stable. Has anyone called the emergency services?'

'I think an ambulance is on its way,' someone told him.

Cooper pulled out his own phone to punch in the three-digit emergency number. They needed more than an ambulance here. Police would be needed to control traffic and spectators. The fire service was needed urgently to stabilise this car with winch lines or something to prevent it getting dislodged by the waves and ending up completely underwater. Even if there were injured people inside the vehicle, it was too dangerous for anyone to try and approach it until it could be secured somehow. Would the hooks and lines from the fire trucks be enough? Maybe they needed to get a crane on the way...

His assessment and planning came to a crunching halt as he got through the rest of the crowd to get a completely clear view of the bottom of the bank. He didn't even finish dialling the emergency services number.

'Hey...' he yelled as loudly as he could. 'What the hell do you think you're *doing*?'

'She just took off down there,' someone said from behind him. 'Seemed like she knew what she was doing...'

'She's mad,' Cooper muttered, staring down at the lone figure on the rocky foreshore a good ten metres beneath him.

The tall, slim woman was standing on top of a rock, a short distance from where the car was teetering on other rocks. She was wearing rolled-up jeans and sneakers, and a white T-shirt that was knotted on one side. Right now, her arms were in the air and she was swiftly winding long dark hair into a knot that she somehow secured easily onto the top of her head. Then she leaned forward, holding her arms out to balance herself, obviously looking for a place to step that would take her closer to the car.

'*Oi...*' Cooper's shout was even louder this time and he was moving as he made the sound. 'Get *back...*'

Sure enough, the ground was crumbling on the edge of the drop and he started a slide that was barely controlled as he aimed for a shrub that had branches big enough to hold his weight. Then he climbed over some rocks and kept going, faster than he knew was safe but he had to get down the bank and into a position where he could stop this crazy bystander from creating yet another problem for the emergency services when they arrived on scene. On top of being concerned about the woman's well-being, he was not happy that he was being forced to put himself in danger like this. As soon as he could, he yelled again.

'Stay where you are. *Wait...*'

She took absolutely no notice of him. With a nimble leap, she landed on another rock and then steadied herself as a wave washed over her feet. Then she moved again to land within reaching distance of the back door of the crashed car. That was when Cooper saw what she was focused on—a small face in the window of that door—a child who looked no more than a couple of years old. He saw her grab the handle of the door and try to open it, almost losing her balance as a larger wave curled around her legs. The door didn't open.

Nobody else was following Cooper down the bank. For a few seconds, when he reached the bottom, he lost sight of what the woman was doing as he scrambled over the rocks closest to the base of the cliff but then reached the point where she had been when he'd first seen her and he had a clear view of what she was up to. She had managed to open the driver's door and he could see the shape of an adult slumped forward, apparently unconscious. The rescuer tilted the person's head back to open the airway, which told Cooper that she did, at least, have some idea of what she was doing, but she didn't pause to do anything else in the way of assessment or treatment for the driver. She slid her arm between the front seat and the back door, twisting her body to enable her to reach the lock, and both the confidence and elegance of her movements kept Cooper standing on his rock, simply watching.

She got the back door open and must have released a safety belt that allowed her to scoop up the small child who was now screaming with terror.

'Mummy… *Mummy*…'

The woman was saying something that Cooper couldn't hear as she wrapped her arms around the child and turned, looking down to choose both her stepping point and a moment when a new wave was not about to break. Cooper moved at the same time, his long stride taking him to the next outcrop of rocks. Someone needed to see what was going on with the child's mother and to try and get her out of the car if it was possible to do so without it being too risky. It wasn't something he would want to try on his own, so it was a relief to hear the sound of sirens getting louder on the road above them. He would make sure this woman and the kid got back safely to shore and then come back to plan the next steps that could be taken the moment the first crews got down the bank.

To his surprise, he found the child being shoved into his arms by the woman. There was nothing he could do but take hold of it.

'Take her,' she said. 'I've got to go back.'

'*No*… It's not safe,' Cooper told her. 'Wait for the firies. That car's not stable.'

'That car has a *baby* in the back seat,' she snapped. 'Keep yourself safe. I've got a job to do, here.'

Cooper was left staring at her back, his jaw slack. He was the person who should be doing whatever was needed here. He had years of experience as an advanced paramedic. Qualifications in scene management and dealing with unusual and dangerous situations just like this. Who was this woman? And what was it about her that made him feel as if she really was the person in charge, here? Did it have anything to do with that hint of something like a grin she'd thrown over her shoulder as she'd turned away from him? Or that he was sure he'd heard her say 'Trust me… I know what I'm doing…'?

The toddler in his arms wriggled and screamed so he held her tightly and carried her carefully out of the water. He could see uniformed fire officers making their way down the bank where a ladder was being positioned. He could also see that the fire truck had been parked so that the winch gear at the back could be deployed. It was going to take a lot more than wedges or chocks to stabilise a car that was rocking on its perch with every wave. There was no sign of an ambulance crew yet. One of the fire officers reached the water's edge at the same time as Cooper. He held his arms out to take the child.

'Is she injured?'

'Haven't checked. Her airway's certainly clear.' And children who were crying that loudly were generally not badly injured. It was more likely to be the quiet ones you had to worry about. 'Are there any medics on scene yet?'

'Not yet. Traffic's snarled up badly for miles. They'll deploy a chopper soon, if it's needed.' The fire officer stared past Cooper. 'How many others are in the car, do you know?'

'Apparently there's a baby in the back. There's a crazy woman who's trying to get her out.' Cooper turned his head but all he could see was an undeniably shapely, denim-clad bottom poking out of the back door of the car. Wriggling, as she moved backwards and then turned, a baby's car seat in her arms.

'Good grief...is that Fizz?' Another fire officer had joined his senior colleague and was shading his eyes against the glint of the afternoon sun on the sea, trying to assess what they were about to deal with.

'Trust her to be first on the scene.' The older fireman shook his head, heading into the water to help rescue the baby. 'Why doesn't it even surprise me?'

'Fizz?' This was getting even weirder, Cooper decided. Who had a name like some sort of party drink?

'She's an ED doc,' he was told. 'But give her a chance to get out in an ambulance or helicopter and she's in, boots 'n all. Everybody in this business knows Fizz.' His tone was admiring. 'Don't worry, she knows what she's doing.' But he was watching the handover of the baby seat to the fire officer. 'Uh-oh...'

'Oh, *no*...' Cooper couldn't believe what he was seeing. There were experts on scene now. Equipment to make any further rescue attempts a lot safer. This woman with the odd name and an unbelievable attitude had already saved two children but it seemed that that wasn't enough. She was heading back to the car yet again.

'Fizz!' the younger fire officer yelled. 'Hold your horses. We need to get a cable onto that car, at least.'

Either she didn't hear him or—and this seemed more likely to Cooper by now—she was choosing not to hear him. He wasn't the only person to be appalled by her recklessness and, as he automatically moved to try and prevent another casualty, he found himself part of a group of rescue workers, armed with ropes and tools and protective clothing. There were police officers here now, as well as the fire crews, but he still couldn't see any paramedics arriving.

'Stay back, mate,' one of them told him. 'This isn't a spectator sport.'

'I'm a paramedic,' Cooper replied. 'With specialty training in disaster and scene management.'

And this looked like it was about to become a disaster, on a small scale, anyway. A wave large enough to reach his waist rolled in and one of the firemen lost his footing. The crashed car also lost its grip on the rocks beneath it, tipping and then sliding sideways with a chilling, metallic screech. A second wave rolled right over the top of its roof.

Where was that adrenaline junkie emergency department doctor?

Cooper couldn't see her anywhere and, just for a heartbeat, he was aware of something that felt like… grief?

He didn't even know this woman and she had taken stupid risks here, so if she was injured or had been killed—perhaps knocked out and then pinned underwater by the car—everybody would know it was her own fault but…

But how incredible a person was she? Cooper had met a lot of courageous people in his lifetime, both as his colleagues and amongst the patients he had treated, but this woman stood out as being something quite astonishing. Fearless. Concerned only about people other than herself.

Or maybe it was something much deeper than that. Much darker. A flashback to a moment in time he could never undo and would never forgive himself for. A moment that he could have used to try harder to stop someone doing something foolhardy. A moment that could have meant he wouldn't have lost the person who'd been everything to him.

A chain of people was in the water now and a plastic basket stretcher was being carried towards where the car had settled, but Cooper was ahead of them and he could see that the driver's door had stayed open as the car had been washed sideways. He could see movement as the foam of a wave cleared. The doctor was still alive…but she was inside the vehicle and it looked like she was struggling to release the catch of the safety belt.

Cooper had a cutting device on his multi-tool that was in a pocket of the first-aid kit he kept in the small backpack but he'd left that back on the beach before he'd climbed that first rock. Because he'd known he wouldn't be able to treat anybody until they were out of the sea. Not that he spared more than a split second of thought to how useful that device would be right now. In fact, he wasn't thinking anything particularly coherent. If he had been, he'd never have done what he did right then, which was to take a deep breath, reach down to take hold of the car door and pull himself beneath the surface of the water.

It was useful to have the outline of the door as a guide because it took more than a second to be able to see past the sting of salt water in his eyes. And it kept him from being washed away by the swirling current of the waves coming past. The car was more stable now than it had been on top of the rocks but it was still moving. How long had it been since the first wave had rolled over its roof and started to fill the interior? How long had it been since this mysterious woman had taken a breath of her own? Her hair had come undone from its knot and was now floating around her head, making her look like a mermaid and probably obscuring her vision as she wrestled with the seat-belt catch.

Cooper caught her hand and pushed it away from the catch. Then he held the bottom and felt for the release button. Pressing it down hard didn't seem to be enough, so he held the button down with one hand and took hold of the upper part of the strap with his other hand and pulled. Hard.

He felt the driver of the car slump towards him as the belt was released and he caught her under her armpits, pulling her free of the vehicle and then pushing up through the water. He just had to hope that she didn't have any kind of spinal injury but there was no way she could have been left in the car long enough for a more careful extrication process because she would have drowned.

He wasn't even sure that she was breathing now as he lifted her head clear of a breaking wave but there were others taking over. Taking the woman from his arms and putting her into the rescue basket to carry her towards the shore. Beside him, his fellow rescuer had already emerged from beneath the surface and she was dragging in great gulps of air as she tried to catch her breath.

'Thanks...' she managed. 'I was having a...bit of trouble...there.'

Not that she looked at all bothered by the fact that her 'bit of trouble' could have actually put them both in danger. She wasn't looking directly at him, either, as she pushed her hair back from her face and swiftly braided it to get it under control but he could see that her whole face had a glow about it—as if it had been so exciting, she'd do it all over again in a heartbeat.

Wow...there was something inspirational in that kind of passion. But Cooper had always known that, hadn't he? She reminded him of...

No. He wasn't about to go there. Even the nudge in that direction was discomforting, which was probably why his tone was distinctly sharp when he spoke again.

'It's lucky I didn't have to rescue you as well,' he said. 'I can't believe you did that.'

The reprimand in his tone was wasted on her. She didn't seem to even be listening. She was watching the progress of the fire officers who were carrying the driver back to shore.

'I need to see if she's okay.' She started moving. 'I'm just hoping...she didn't start drowning while I was fiddling with that belt.'

'There was still some air in there, between waves.' Cooper automatically reached out as the woman beside him stumbled on a rock. To his surprise, she caught his hand and held it as they both made their way back to shore as quickly as they could. His brain registered how that wet T-shirt was clinging to her body and he knew that image was going to resurface at a later, and less inappropriate, moment.

They were both soaking wet and should have been freezing given the water temperature and the slight breeze adding a chill factor but, oddly, the only thing that made Cooper realise he might be cold was the extraordinary warmth of that hand he was holding. It wasn't until she let go, as they leapt out of the last wash of the waves, that he started to shiver.

The toddler and the baby in the car seat were no-where to be seen so they must have been taken up the bank already. Perhaps the police officers on scene were caring for them in the warmth of one of their vehicles. They needed to get the female driver into shelter as well but it looked as if she wasn't stable enough for what would have to be a slow journey up the steep slope.

He watched Fizz crouch beside the woman. She had her cheek near the victim's face and a hand on her abdomen. 'She's breathing…just.' She looked past the group of fire officers nearby. 'Doesn't look like we've got an ambulance on scene yet, does it?'

'No.' Cooper could see his own backpack not that far away. 'But I'm a paramedic. I've got a kit. I'll grab a stethoscope, shall I?'

It was the first really direct look he had received from her. She had brown eyes, he noticed. Really dark orbs that were assessing him with lightning speed.

'Get my kit, too, would you?' she said. 'It's over there on top of that flat rock.'

Cooper moved instantly. It felt as if he'd passed an

unspoken test of some kind, he realised as he grabbed both backpacks and turned back. Not that it should have made any difference at all to this situation but instinct told him that it would not be an easy thing to gain this woman's approval. Absurdly, Cooper actually felt a beat of pride in himself that he was being accepted as a temporary colleague.

He was a big bear of a man, this unexpected assistant that she had. Well over six feet in height and broad-shouldered.

Felicity Wilson believed that he was what he said he was. He'd clearly known what he was doing when he'd taken over getting this woman out of her crashed car and the way he'd told her to stay back until the car could be secured safely was pretty much what most people in the emergency services would have told her.

How could anybody have stood back when you could see that tiny face in the window, though? And yeah… Fizz knew she had a bit of an issue with impulsiveness when it came to dangerous situations but how good did it feel when taking that risk actually worked?

It would feel even better if she could make sure the mother of those children made it out of this disaster alive.

He had big hands as well, this man, but they were clever and nimble. He was opening pockets within the backpacks and extracting all the kinds of things that were going to be needed. Fizz stole the occasional glance as she looked up from doing a rapid primary survey on her patient, who was groaning but not conscious enough to open her eyes or speak to them coherently. She lay in the plastic rescue basket the fire service had provided.

Currently, those officers were setting up a canvas wind shield around them and watching what was happening. Two of them had taken off their heavy jackets and had passed them to the medics. Fizz felt swamped by the size of the garment but she wasn't about to let it hamper her movements.

'I'd put her GCS at less than ten. She's tachycardic at one twenty-four,' she told the man helping to stabilise her patient. 'Tachypnoeic with a respiration rate of thirty-two and… I'm not sure I'm getting any breath sounds on the left side. Hard to tell with the noise of the waves.'

'Pneumothorax?' The fire-service jacket looked like it was the perfect size for this man. And he looked as if he was well used to a uniform and the authority it conveyed. He had found the small oxygen cylinder in a side pocket of her first-aid kit and was attaching a mask. 'Is she hypoxic?'

'Let's get some oxygen on.' Fizz nodded. 'Got some shears?' She cut at the woman's clothing when he placed the tool in her hands and then slipped the elastic of the oxygen mask around their patient's head to keep it in place.

'Look at that…' The marks of deep bruising from the seat-belt injury were already visible in dark red patches. Fizz palpated the side of the woman's chest. 'Definitely some rib fractures.'

Her partner had his fingers on the woman's neck. 'Carotid pulse palpable but weak,' he told her. 'Looks like her jugular venous pressure is raised, too.'

Fizz nodded. She could see the veins on the neck

were visibly distended. She needed to have another listen to the chest and to check whether the tracheal line was deviated, which could confirm that air trapped in the woman's chest was developing into the emergency that a tension pneumothorax represented.

Her partner was setting up for an IV, she noticed. He had his own roll that contained cannulas, alcohol wipes, Luer plugs and tape. He also had a litre of saline and a giving set ready to go. And he'd got a blood-pressure cuff on their patient's arm already.

'Blood pressure's eighty-five over fifty,' he told her. 'Can't see any external bleeding. I'll check that her pelvis is stable in a tick.'

Fizz nodded but didn't say anything for a moment. She had her stethoscope on her patient's chest. Right side then left side. Yes…she was sure there were no breath sounds on the left but was it air or blood that was stopping the lung functioning?

'I'm missing my ED ultrasound,' she muttered.

'The portable ones we carry in the ambulance now are great. Love them.'

She gave him a glance that probably looked startled but she knew that it was only the most highly trained paramedics that got to use equipment like portable ultrasound machines or ventilators. This guy not only knew what he was doing but he was very likely to be very good at it as well. It only took the briefest eye contact but she knew that he could tell exactly what she was thinking. His gaze was steady.

I am good at what I do, it told her. *You can trust me…*

'What's your name?'

'Cooper. Cooper Sinclair.'

He wasn't local. Fizz would have noticed this man amongst all the emergency services personnel she had worked with in the last few years. Noticed and remembered him. It wasn't just his size that made him stand out. He had a strong Scottish accent. Not that where he came from or why he was here was of any interest to her right now.

'What do you need there, Doc?' A senior fire officer had come close. 'Ambulance is just arriving on scene now but it'll take them a minute or two to get their gear down the cliff. They want me to ask you what you need.'

'The usual,' Fizz responded. 'Life pack, oxygen and the kit. I'd like to get her airway secured before we move her.'

'Her name's Sonya Greene. We got her bag out of the car and found her driver's licence. She's thirty-two years old.'

The same age as she was. With two very young children. 'Somebody tracing next of kin?'

'Cops are onto it. I'll go and help get that gear down to you.'

'You going to intubate?' Cooper asked as the fire officer stepped back, talking into his radio.

'I'll need to decompress the chest before intubating.'

He nodded. 'Positive pressure ventilation could make a pneumothorax a lot worse.'

'I think it's getting worse, anyway. Does that look like tracheal deviation to you?'

His head came very close to her own as he leaned over to get into a position to be able to see the line of their patient's neck and chest. Fizz could feel his body heat, which struck her as odd because she knew how cold they both had to be, despite the thick jackets over their wet clothes. She made a note in the corner of her brain that they should probably wrap some foil sheets around themselves at the first opportunity. But she wasn't going to mention it just yet. Somehow, she knew that this Cooper was not going to be any more interested in his own protection from hypothermia at the moment than she was.

'Yeah,' he said. 'Tension pneumothorax?'

'That's what I'm thinking.'

The new medics on scene arrived moments later.

'Want me to get an IV in, Fizz?' one of the paramedics asked.

'We're good for the moment. You've got that, haven't you, Cooper?'

'Yep.'

It was someone else's turn to look startled. Fizz gave him a brief nod. 'Cooper here is an advanced paramedic, Jack,' she told the new arrival. 'I was lucky he was here. We nearly didn't get to save this woman. And right now, I need to decompress her chest and I want to do a finger thoracostomy rather than a needle decompression. Can you draw up some local?' She looked at the second crew member. 'Could you get the monitor on, please? I'd like to know what her oxygen and CO_2 levels are.'

All four of them were kept very busy for the next fifteen minutes but Fizz was satisfied that it was safe to transport their patient by that point. The chest decompression had dealt with the breathing emergency and both the pulse and breathing rate had dropped to an acceptable level. Blood pressure was coming up and the airway was controlled.

'Good job.' She nodded, as the paramedics secured their patient in the basket for the journey up the steep bank. 'I'll come with you in the ambulance and get a police officer to get my car back into town.'

There were plenty of fire officers ready to help lift the basket stretcher and pass it up the chain of people on the bank. Fizz shoved things back into her pack and zipped it shut. She could tidy and restock it at the hospital. Cooper was collecting his own kit.

'Thanks for your help,' she told him. 'Couldn't have done it without you.'

'It was a pleasure.' Cooper smiled at her and, to her surprise, Fizz found her breath actually catching in her throat.

Wow…that was some smile…

'Yeah…thanks, mate.' Jack, the paramedic, was slipping the straps of his large pack over his shoulders. 'You here on holiday or something?'

'No. I'm actually starting work here tomorrow. At the Aratika Rescue Base?'

'Oh, wow…choppers?'

'And the rest.' Cooper's shrug was modest. 'Coastguard work. Police operations. Specialist Emergency Response Team stuff.'

The glance Jack threw over his shoulder, as he went to catch up with the progress of the stretcher, was impressed.

Fizz had to admit she was pretty impressed herself. The members of that team on the rescue base were an elite group of people. She'd love to be an official, full-time member of that team herself but she loved her hospital work too much to give it up. Right now, she had arranged her life to give her the best of both worlds, by devoting her spare time away from ED shifts to the base and she got to work with some amazing people in both arenas.

It looked as if a new and very interesting person had just arrived in one of her worlds.

'Guess I'll be seeing you around,' she told Cooper. 'I try to be available to help on as many shifts as I can with the base.'

'Good to know,' he said. 'I'll be able to find out the end of this story. I hope it's a happy ending.'

'I specialise in happy endings wherever possible.' Fizz threw him a grin as she headed towards the bank. The stretcher was more than halfway up already. They would be on the road and heading for the biggest emergency department in the area within a few minutes.

She turned her head once more as she stepped onto the first rung of the ladder that was now secured to the bank.

Cooper wasn't that far behind her.

'Hey,' he called.

'What?'

'Just wanted to say that your name suits you. See you around, Fizz.'

She didn't say anything in response. She didn't look back again as she climbed to road level and then into the back of the ambulance. It was time to put the big, Scottish paramedic right out of her mind and focus on keeping her patient stable until they reached the hospital and got her to Theatre, if necessary, as quickly as possible to sort out that chest injury.

Fizz knew she would see him around sooner or later.

Hopefully, it would be sooner...

CHAPTER TWO

'IT'S A FANTASTIC LOCATION.'

Cooper was standing in front of the glass wall that made up this central, third-floor office area of the Aratika Rescue Base. He could see the helipad directly below them with people working around two bright yellow aircraft. It looked as if one of the helicopters was being refuelled and someone—presumably a pilot—was walking around the other one, doing a detailed external check.

'They're Kawasaki BK117s, yes?'

'With every bell and whistle you could wish for.' Aratika's manager, Don Smith, sounded proud. 'We've got a backup Squirrel in case both the BKs are out at the same time and there's no way of getting to another job by road or sea, but that's actually never happened during my time here.' He rapped his knuckles on the window sill. 'Touch wood. If I needed saving I'd want it to be a BK showing up. They're awesome rescue aircraft.'

'They're exactly what we used at the base in Scotland. Love working in them.'

'You'll be very familiar with the layout, then, which

is a bonus. How many years have you got under your belt now? Ten?'

'Close enough. I got into helicopter work as soon as I could after I graduated as a paramedic. It was always my burning ambition. Ever since I saw a crew at work when I was a teenager, up in a mountain range in Scotland.'

But it hadn't been the overwhelming relief of seeing the helicopter arrive at that accident scene that had instilled an unwavering determination to be like the members of that crew. It hadn't even been the astonishingly technical level of care that had been provided for the victim of that horrendous fall that had made him feel like he was in an episode of some high drama medical television series. No…what had stayed with Cooper and made him so determined to be like those heroes had been the way *he* had been cared for. The absolute compassion in the way they had done their best to support him as he'd dealt with the horror of his brother's death and the respect they had shown to both himself and to Connor—even after they knew there was nothing more they could do for him.

'And you've added a string of other accomplishments as well.' Don's words cut into the memory that had flashed into his mind. 'I have to say your CV was pretty impressive. Urban and Land Search and Rescue qualifications, with mountain experience. Disaster management. Coastguard training…'

Cooper shrugged modestly. 'I like to keep busy. And I like the challenge of learning new stuff. Or being in a new environment—and from what I've seen of New Zealand so far, it's got a lot to offer.'

He knew how impressive his CV was but there was

a downside to the kind of ambition that had driven him to achieve so much in his career already. It came from a single-minded devotion to that career that had meant there'd been no room for anything else in his life. Here he was in his mid-thirties—all of twenty years since his determination to be the best rescue worker ever had been conceived—and there'd been nothing to hold him back from shifting his life to the other side of the world for a fresh and interesting challenge.

No long-term relationship to consider. No family ties that were binding. No desire for family ties like that, for that matter. Cooper Sinclair lived for his work and, yeah...the downside was that it could be lonely sometimes, but he wouldn't have that impressive CV or be as good at this job as he knew his references recorded if he'd let a personal life interfere with where he was heading. Or maybe that should be where he'd already arrived. Was that why he'd come in search of new challenges in a new country? Because he'd been running out of ideas of how to take his skill set to an even higher level?

He shifted his gaze to a parking area off to one side of the helipad, where there were four-wheel drive emergency vehicles, huge command centre trucks and even rescue service motorbikes parked.

'You're well equipped to respond by road. And did I read that you take charge of any major incidents?'

Don nodded. 'We get dispatched to work with police and the fire service as command for any multiple casualty incidents or disasters. We also have single-crewed vehicles available at all times for first response if the local ambulance service is overloaded or they need advanced paramedic assistance for patient care.

Those staff members are in addition to the helicopter crews. That's where we're starting you off for orientation.'

Cooper's eyebrows rose even though he tilted his head to acknowledge the challenge. But Don smiled.

'Don't worry. We're not throwing you in the deep end by yourself just yet. You'll be double-crewed until you are comfortable with protocols and destinations, etcetera. In fact...' Don checked his watch. 'Let's head downstairs. Shift changeover will be happening and there'll be a good crowd to introduce you to, including the guy who's going to be crewed with you for the moment. I expect they'll all be having breakfast right now.'

'Sounds great.' Cooper took one more look at the stunning view of Wellington harbour in front of him with the skyline of the city visible to one side, past the cranes and ships of a busy port and rugged, forest-covered hills in the distance to the other side. 'I still can't get over this view,' he said as he followed his new manager. 'You must have one of the best offices in the world.'

'Can't complain,' Don agreed. 'But this location was chosen for more than the view it gives us upstairs. It provides the fastest access to pretty much everywhere we need to go. We've got a straight run into the central city, or over to the west coast, we've got the coastguard base two minutes away when they need a medic, and if we're heading to the mountains or further north, the choppers just head straight for those hills, which is well away from the flight paths for the airport. That's where the name came from. Aratika means a direct, or straight, path in Maori.'

'Great name.' Cooper let the door swing shut on the view behind him.

There was an enticing smell of frying bacon coming from the kitchen area of the staffroom on the second floor of this big, modern building and, due to the change of a night shift to a day shift, there was a large enough group of people to present a challenge in remembering all the names coming at Cooper. Paramedics, pilots, ground crew, which included mechanics and people that serviced and restocked gear—even an older woman who seemed to have the role of a housekeeper—Shirley. It was Shirley who was cooking the bacon at the moment.

'Welcome to Aratika,' she said to Cooper, with a warm smile. 'Can I interest you in a bacon sandwich?'

'Thanks…maybe later.' Cooper wasn't ready to relax enough to eat yet but everybody here seemed just as welcoming as Shirley, so far. It was disconcerting, a moment after thinking that, to find someone staring at him, their jaw dropping.

'No way…' He looked back at the newspaper spread on the table in front of him, flipping back to the front page.

'That's Joe,' Don told him. 'He's the one you'll be double-crewing with until you're comfortable with how things work around here. Joe? This is Cooper Sinclair.'

'And unless he's got an identical twin brother…' Joe looked up again as he got to his feet. 'I've been looking at a picture of what you were getting up to yesterday afternoon. You just couldn't wait to get to work, huh?'

'Oh?' Cooper's smile froze halfway. It was a just a throwaway comment on behalf of his new colleague.

There was no was Joe could know that he'd touched a deep nerve.

That Cooper *had* had an identical twin brother...

Joe gestured at the newspaper. 'You're a hero already.'

Cooper hadn't seen any newspapers yet today. Or any television last night, for that matter. By the time he'd got through the traffic jam the accident had created and located the central city hotel that would be home until he found something more permanent, he'd been too wrecked to do anything but sort out his wet clothing, find something to eat and then crash for the night. At least he'd been able to contact Don and apologise for missing his orientation meeting at the base and it had been a relief to find that his new manager hadn't been fazed.

'Tomorrow's another day,' he'd said. 'Can't fault you for getting involved in an accident scene. Would have been disappointed if you hadn't.'

Joe was looking just as laid back as he held out his hand. 'Good to meet you, Cooper. Look forward to working with you.'

Cooper shook his hand. 'Likewise.'

Don was reaching for the paper. 'Front page? Oh... Nice photo...'

Someone had taken it from the top of the cliff with a good zoom lens. There he was, with that crying toddler in his arms, facing back towards the shore. Just a little out of focus in the background behind him, he could see Fizz heading back to where the car was teetering on the rocks, a splash of foam catching the sunlight dramatically in mid-air like a halo around both the vehicle and the woman.

'Looks like you were enjoying yourself, mate.' One of the pilots had stepped closer to look over Don's shoulder.

'I wouldn't say that, exactly,' Cooper murmured, but he had to admit there was a hint of something other than professional concern in his expression and he knew why as well.

That had been the moment when he'd been processing the way Fizz had dismissed his bid of taking charge of the situation. When she'd turned back to go and get the baby. When she'd cracked a version of what had become an old joke—*Trust me... I'm a doctor...* He'd been gobsmacked but undeniably impressed. Maybe that was the reason for that hint of a lopsided smile on his face and yes…it did look as if it could be interpreted as him getting an enormous amount of satisfaction out of what he was doing. It was just as well, he thought, that the picture hadn't been taken a bit later, when they'd been holding hands as they'd hopped rocks to get back to shore—their wet clothes plastered against their skin.

He'd been right about that particular image coming back to haunt him. It had happened when he'd stood for a long time under the spray of that very welcome hot shower. It had come back with even more punch when he'd slid, naked, between the crisp sheets of his bed. If she ever got tired of being some kind of action woman, Fizz could probably easily get a job as a model. Tall and slim but with curves in all the right places. That long dark hair, dark eyes and olive skin that made him think she could have Mediterranean ancestry. Greek or Italian, maybe?

'I heard about that job. I was in the ED when it came in.'

Cooper turned towards the speaker, relieved to have his runaway thoughts reined in so abruptly. It was a petite woman with blonde hair who was about his own age. What was her name again? Oh, yeah… Maggie.

'Do you know if the patient was still stable on arrival? I think her name was Sonya. And if the kids were okay?'

'Yep.' Maggie nodded. 'I was around for a while. I'd gone in with a kid from up north who was in status asthmaticus and I wanted to hang around until he was stable. I'm pretty sure the kids were fine. They got checked out and there were relatives to take care of them, including their father from what I gathered. They put a chest drain in the mother, took off about a litre of blood and fluid, gave her a blood transfusion and then took her off to Theatre. I don't know what they needed to do to patch her up, though. You can ask Fizz next time she's here. She went with her to Theatre.'

'Fizz?' Someone else, a bacon sandwich in hand, paused to peer at the picture. 'Oh, for heaven's sake… that's her in the background, isn't it?'

'She was the first on scene,' Cooper said. 'I was yelling at her to stay back until the car could be stabilised but she didn't take a blind bit of notice.'

'Sounds like Fizz.' But Joe was grinning. 'You'll find she behaves better when she's in uniform.' His grin broadened. 'Sometimes.'

The familiarity in his tone gave Cooper an odd beat of something he didn't want to try and identify but could be related to envy, perhaps? Just how well did Joe know Fizz? And why was he even wondering about whether she was single or not? For heaven's sake, he'd only just arrived in a new city to start a new job and a new life. Hooking up with someone hadn't even entered his head as part of his immediate agenda. To contemplate the remote possibility of hooking up with someone he'd only spent a matter of minutes with, not to mention someone who'd pretty much ignored him to start with, who'd bossed him around like a minion after that, and had probably forgotten his existence the moment she'd walked away was…well, it was stupid enough to make it easy to dismiss in the same instant it had grazed his mind.

Don's smile was tolerant enough to suggest that he, too, not only knew Fizz well but could excuse her lack of compliance with safety instructions. His expression reminded Cooper of a fond parent who made allowances for a wayward child. The attitude to the young doctor was intriguing. What did she have that made everybody who knew her prepared to forgive what came across as a maverick streak—something that was not usually acceptable in the emergency services community?

Don had already moved on from his amusement in relation to how well Fizz behaved herself when she was officially on duty. 'Speaking of uniforms, we need to get Cooper here kitted out. Although…' His gaze took in the black T-shirt, dark trousers and steel-capped boots Cooper was wearing. 'Just a team T-shirt might be enough for the moment. And some overalls for a chopper callout, maybe. If there's room, he could go as third crew at some point soon. He definitely needs

a pager, though. Preferably before your shift is due
to start.'

'Come on…' Joe signalled that Cooper should follow him. 'I'll introduce you to Danny downstairs
who's in charge of uniforms and pagers and suchlike
and then we'll find you a locker. The grand tour can
wait until after breakfast if things stay quiet for that
long.'

Even as he finished speaking, a loud beeping was
heard and one of the pilots reached for his pager.
Two of the paramedics, including Maggie, reached
for theirs seconds later. All three staff members got
to their feet and headed for the stairway that led to
ground level.

Maggie wagged her finger at Joe as she went past.
'That was your fault,' she told him. 'You said the "Q"
word. Karma's going to get you soon, as well, you
know.'

'She's right.' Joe sighed. 'We'd better sort your
pager out first, Cooper. We'll be the next taxi in the
rank before long. Let's get you that pair of overalls
until we sort your full uniform out properly.'

'Phew…' Felicity Wilson let herself sink into the arm-
chair in the corner of the emergency department staffroom of Wellington's Royal Hospital. 'I thought we
were never going to get a break.'

'It's been full on, hasn't it? Thanks for staying on,
Fizz, but you can get away anytime now. We're fully
staffed for the afternoon shift and we've caught up
on the backlog.'

'I'll just have my coffee and catch my breath.' Fizz
smiled at her colleague, Tom—one of the senior con-

sultants here. 'I've already ditched my plans to attend a four-wheel drive club meeting. They're just planning the next run, which is a sand forest gig that I've done before. I might wait until the CT scan results come through on that six-year-old kid that fell out of the tree. I hope he hasn't got anything more than a mild concussion to go with his broken arm.'

'Young Micky? He's been a frequent flyer in here since he was a toddler when he fell off the couch and broke his collarbone. Apparently that was his first attempt at flying.' Tom shook his head. 'You have to feel sorry for his mother.' His glance at Fizz was accompanied by a grin. 'I'll bet your mother had that worried look a lot of the time when you were growing up.'

'I wasn't accident prone.'

'But you're into dangerous pastimes. You probably jumped out of trees with a homemade parachute instead of falling out of them.'

'Actually, no… I was quite a boring kid. Very well behaved.'

Tom shook his head. 'So what happened? You grew up and just got a taste for things like hang gliding and off-road driving?'

Fizz shrugged. 'Something like that.' Yeah…she'd got a taste for an overdose of adrenaline, that was true. Who wouldn't, when you discovered that it could blow anything else that you were feeling into oblivion?

Things like grief.

And having no faith in the future.

Mind you, it was such a long time ago that she'd discovered the potency of adrenaline as a mood-altering medication it was just a part of her history. A life-changing part, admittedly, especially when she'd eventually found a way of incorporating that kind of excitement into the job she loved so much. At least people were more likely to be impressed when you were putting yourself in danger in order to save other people and not just for personal escape masquerading as enjoyment.

'And you always just happen to be where the action is happening. That picture of you in the paper a few days ago… Unbelievable… And you just happened to be driving right behind the woman who ran her car off the road?'

'I saw it happening. Some idiot on a motorbike was trying to pass when he didn't have room and she had to swerve. Her wheel caught in the gravel on the side of the road and she just lost control and went straight through the barrier.' Fizz shrugged. 'Hey…what can I say? Apparently I'm a trauma magnet.'

'I guess it keeps life interesting.'

'Yep…' Fizz took a sip of her coffee, her mind slipping back to that incident the other day. To the adrenaline rush of getting that child and the baby out of that car. To that moment of fear when she'd been underwater and realising that she wasn't going to get that safety belt undone and that, at any moment, the car could get displaced enough to trap her underwater.

She was no stranger to situations that were scary. She had chosen them, way back, when it hadn't actually seemed to matter that much if she didn't survive. By the time she'd got through to the other side of the darkest period in her life, she had every desire to survive but she still didn't shy away from situations that she knew might be a little too risky, because she knew how good that rush of relief was when they were over.

That sheer exhilaration that the odds had been beaten and you were still alive? It was definitely a kind of drug, that feeling.

Addictive...

And every time it added to her confidence in being able to rely on herself. It confirmed her belief that being totally independent was the only safe way to exist and it was okay, because life was still good. Better than good, in fact.

'Anyway... I'd better get back.' Tom drained his mug and then rinsed it out under the tap. 'You in tomorrow, Fizz?'

'No. Day off.'

'As in a real day off, or are you doing a shift at the rescue base?'

'Rescue base,' Fizz admitted. 'But you know what they say about a change being as good as a holiday, right?'

Tom was laughing as he left the staffroom. Fizz sipped her coffee again, her gaze drifting towards the big table in the centre of the room and to the pile of magazines and newspapers on one end of it.

It had only been a couple of days since she'd been in the background of that front-page picture. Was the paper still in that pile? Not that Fizz kept mementoes like that but, now that Tom had reminded her, she just wanted to have another look at that photo.

It wasn't until she'd found the paper on the bottom of the pile that Fizz realised why she'd wanted to see it again. There was something about the man who was the hero of this image that was pulling her back.

Attracting her...

And it had been a long time since she'd been aware

of that particular kind of tingle. Had her self-imposed break from men gone on long enough to have run its course? Was she missing male companionship—not to mention great sex—enough to make it worth the risk of having to deal with someone who started wanting something more than she was prepared to offer?

More than she was capable of offering?

Maybe the attraction was simply there because they'd shared a dramatic incident and he'd been the one to tip the balance and make the good result of that rescue possible. Fizz could still feel echoes from that touch of his hand when he'd pushed hers aside to deal with unclipping that seat belt. And when he'd gripped hers to help her keep her balance when they'd been scrambling over those slippery rocks on their way back to dry land. How safe had that physical attachment to that big, solid man made her feel? Not that she needed anyone to make her feel safe but it hadn't been unpleasant, that was for sure.

She could remember how deft his hands had been when he had been working with her to save that woman's life on the beach. And that hint of laughter curling through a rather gorgeous accent when he'd said that her name suited her. It wasn't just Cooper Sinclair's accent that was gorgeous, either. Fizz stared at the photo. She'd noticed how big he was that day but she hadn't taken any particular notice of his features—those intelligent eyes, that strong nose and chin. A mouth that looked ready to curl into what would probably be a cheeky smile at any moment.

Okay. The attraction wasn't just to do with the situation they had both found themselves in. And it wasn't just that she was over being celibate. This Cooper was something special. He was also a foreigner who might only be in the country for a limited amount of time, which could be a real bonus. If—and, given the impression she already had of him, it might be quite a big if—he was single, it was possible he might be interested in a friendship. One of those friendships that had benefits, even, and were as close to a conventional relationship as Fizz was prepared to allow.

She cast a somewhat furtive glance over her shoulder but she was still alone in the staffroom. Carefully, she ripped off the front page of this old newspaper and then folded and tore around the edges of that photograph. Then she folded the image until it became a small square that she slipped into the pocket of her scrubs tunic.

It was an odd thing to do but…she might want to have another look at it later. When she wasn't in danger of being interrupted.

CHAPTER THREE

'HI, COOPER, HOW'S it going?'

'Hey, Maggie… I didn't know you rode a bike.' Cooper shut the door of his SUV, which he'd parked in the corner of the staff parking area at Aratika Base, well away from any rescue vehicles and especially the big trucks that might need to exit the park quickly.

'It's what helped me get a job here, I think.' Maggie tucked her helmet under her arm and fell into step beside Cooper as they headed for the ground-floor entrance on one side of the helicopter hangar. 'We can rotate sometimes if we need a change or there's a gap that needs filling in the roster—that's why Joe's on the road crewing with you at the moment. He'll probably be back on the choppers next week.' Maggie used her security card to open a steel door. 'I love spending a few shifts on a bike. If there's a major snarl-up in traffic due to a crash, a bike is the best way to get on scene fast. We can respond first and do what we can before the police can clear a way in for an ambulance or find somewhere for a chopper to land.'

'I haven't ridden a bike for a few years. Maybe I'd better brush up on my skills.'

'Good thinking. I see you've got an SUV, though. Do you do some off-road four-wheel driving?'

'Not yet. Could be a fun thing to get into here. There must be some great places to go.'

'I've been out with Fizz. She belongs to a big four-by-four club and they have days where they get onto some farms with steep gullies and rivers to get across. Or they get into a forest near a beach so there's sand dunes and things to deal with. It's a bit hair-raising but pretty exciting.' Maggie was leading the way into the ground-floor locker room. 'It's also a great way to pick up driving skills. I should do more of it. Oh… I had a chat to my other flatmates, Laura and Jack, last night and told them you might be interested in our spare room. They're keen, so come and have a look after work today, if you like.'

'That would be fantastic. I'm not into hotel living. A few days has been more than enough.' Cooper put his gym bag into his locker and shut the door. He was already wearing his uniform and the overalls for helicopter or other callouts were hanging on his hook at the end of the row on the wall.

'It's a cool old house. Big villa. It's in the Aro Valley, which isn't too far from here. Less than a fifteen-minute drive even if the traffic isn't great.'

'Sounds great.'

'We're all either paramedics or nurses so, with our shift work, it means it's not that much of an issue that we've only got one bathroom. We're hardly ever all there at the same time. There is one thing you should probably know, though…'

'What's that?' Cooper had been distracted by someone coming through the door of the changing room.

Fizz…

He hadn't seen her since the day before he'd started work on the base and that was nearly a week ago. Long enough for him to have got over that odd reaction and the even crazier notion that maybe there was a possibility they could hook up.

'Hi, Maggie…' Fizz was walking with a confidence that said she knew exactly where her locker was. That she was completely at home here, in fact. 'And…um… Cooper, isn't it?'

'Yeah…'

Had she had trouble remembering his name? The effect of the hesitation was not dissimilar to having a bucket of cold water thrown at him. So much for thinking that there might have been a mutual spark of attraction there.

'Cooper Sinclair,' he added. 'We never did get properly introduced, did we? Your real name isn't actually Fizz, is it?'

'Don't go there.' Maggie laughed. 'Her real name is Felicity and she hates it. You won't be popular if you try using it.'

There was a slight flush of colour on Fizz's cheeks and she barely held eye contact with Cooper for more than a heartbeat. As if she was a little flustered, perhaps? He might not really know this woman at all, but instinct told him that being flustered was out of character for this woman. Interesting. And, no, he wasn't going to make himself instantly unpopular by using a name she didn't like but, for the moment, he was certainly going to keep any interaction between them completely professional. Because instinct was also telling him that if he came on too strong, he would get a very firm knock back.

'I heard you went up to Theatre with our patient from that accident the other day,' he said. 'Sonya?'

'I did.' Fizz was opening her locker but it wasn't to find any uniform items. She was already wearing the black T-shirt with the rescue base's logo of a helicopter flying above a path leading straight towards a mountain range and she had it tucked into the standard issue black pants that brushed the top of her steel-capped boots. With her hair firmly drawn back and tamed into a long braid, she looked ready to leap into a car or a helicopter and respond to any emergency. She hung her big shoulder bag on a hook in the locker, having extracted a stethoscope, notebook, pens and a couple of muesli bars as she continued talking to Cooper.

'She lost a lot of blood when we got a chest tube in so she needed a transfusion. They did a thoracostomy in Theatre and found some small arteries that were still bleeding so they got repaired, along with the lung damage.'

'Is she still in hospital?'

'No. She went to the intensive care unit, got extubated the next day. The chest tube got taken out forty-eight hours later and she was discharged yesterday.'

'Wow...good to hear.' Cooper was impressed. Not just that their patient was recovering so quickly from both the injury and the surgery but that Fizz had clearly kept a very close eye on her progress. 'Do you always follow your patients up that closely?'

'Try to...'

Fizz slung her stethoscope around her neck and looked even more ready to respond to anything. She also looked as if she either had no interest in continuing this conversation or couldn't think of anything to say. There was a moment's silence that could have become awkward if Maggie hadn't broken it.

'Cooper might be moving into the spare room at my place,' Maggie told Fizz. 'Except he doesn't know about Harrison yet.'

'Harrison?' It was a relief for Cooper to turn towards Maggie and stop wondering why there was any awkwardness in the atmosphere. 'Is he a flat pet?'

Maggie laughed. 'Kind of. One of the housemates is Laura, who's an ED nurse at the Royal, and she's a single mum. Harrison is five. He's no trouble and they share the biggest room in the house that's got an ensuite bathroom. It just depends on how you feel about kids.'

'I'm fine with kids,' Cooper said. His mouth curved into a grin. 'I like them. As long as they're not mine, that is.'

'You don't like your own kids?' Fizz shut her locker door with a decisive clunk and shot him a glance from beneath raised eyebrows.

'Don't have any,' he responded. 'And don't intend to in the foreseeable future, anyway.'

Maggie let out an audible sigh. 'What is it with the men around here? Nobody seems to want to settle down and have a family. Not just the men, either,' she added. 'Seems like half the staff here are single. Look at me—I'm thirty-five. If I don't get on with something soon, it's never going to happen.'

'Ah...but would you want to give up this job?' Fizz slung her arm around Maggie's shoulders as they both walked towards a steel staircase. 'Imagine how boring it might be to be stuck at home with a few rug rats. You won't catch me doing that...'

'You're only thirty-two, aren't you? Just you wait, Fizz. Your biological clock will start ticking one of these days.'

Fizz laughed. 'Doubt it. And if it does, I'm going to ignore it. Life's too much fun just the way it is.'

Cooper was just behind them as they headed up to the first floor and the staff area. The contrast between these two women was quite startling. Maggie was very attractive with her curly blonde hair and blue eyes. He'd been out as third crew on a helicopter call-out with her on his second day here, so he'd seen her at work and knew that her intelligence and skills more than made up for any lack of height or brute strength. She rode a Harley-Davidson motorbike, which gave her an edge that should have added to her attractiveness, and it sounded like she was looking for someone special in her life.

Maggie should be exactly the type of woman that would be perfect for Cooper—if he was looking, of course—which he wasn't.

But when Maggie was standing beside Fizz, she seemed to become pale and it wasn't just her colouring against Fizz's dark hair and eyes and olive skin. It was as if her personality paled as well, to the point of being almost insipid? Cooper knew that wasn't the case, it was just that Fizz had an extraordinary kind of glow about her. She was a maverick, all right. Clearly she wasn't about to bow to any social pressure any more than she was inclined to automatically follow orders regarding safety. She wasn't looking for a conventional future of finding a partner and settling down to raise a family. Instead, she was throwing herself at life and extracting all the fun she could out of it. And if that meant throwing caution to the wind and doing things that were reckless, then so be it.

She was a bit wild.

And that wasn't just attractive, it was undeniably exciting. It felt as if the aura around this woman was touching his own skin. Making it tingle oddly. No wonder he'd been aware of awkwardness between them—he was creating it. Not that Cooper was going to allow even a hint of his reaction to show. The fact that Fizz had barely remembered his name was quite enough for self-protection barriers to have been engaged instantly. He wasn't about to make an idiot of himself in front of his new colleagues. *With* one of his new colleagues, in fact, even though her presence on the base was intermittent.

Oh, man...

It was a relief to get into the staffroom with the group of friendly, familiar faces. Enough people to dilute how powerful the presence of Cooper Sinclair was when he was breathing the same air that Fizz was. He was too big. Too cute. Too...*everything*...

It was disturbing, that's what it was.

'Fizz...how are you, love?' Shirley was calling from where she was standing in front of the stove. 'It's poached eggs on toast this morning. Can I tempt you?'

'Oh, yes, please, Shirley. You're an angel. I went for a run this morning and there was no time to do more than grab a couple of these muesli bars.' She held out her hand to reveal her snacks.

'Keep those for later. Sit down and I'll bring you some eggs. Maggie? Cooper? You up for eggs?'

'No, thanks,' Maggie said. 'I've had my breakfast.' She went towards the big pine board on the wall behind the dining table, where Don was pinning up a notice. 'Is that the new roster?' she asked.

'I'd love some,' Cooper said to Shirley at the same time. 'I went running this morning, too, and I'm starving.'

Oh, no... If Shirley had asked Cooper first, then Fizz might have lied and said she'd already eaten breakfast as well. But now he was sitting beside her at the table and, any moment now, they'd be eating a meal together, albeit a snatched one before their shift was due to start. Joe was also sitting at the table, along with Andy, one of their pilots, and a couple of paramedics from the night shift. She was more than familiar with sitting down with team members from this rescue base. It shouldn't feel any different with the inclusion of someone new. But it did. And Fizz knew why.

It was entirely her own fault that she was feeling a bit...well, weird, around Cooper Sinclair. She'd looked at that newspaper clipping a few times too often, hadn't she? Remembering his voice and that cute Scottish accent. The sheer, solid size of him that made her feel quite small and feminine, which was no mean feat for a girl who'd reached nearly six feet by the time she was sixteen. She'd remembered too often how it had felt to have him holding her hand as well and that had morphed into imagining a whole lot more by the time she was lying awake in her own bed in the early hours of the mornings. The idea that a friendship might be possible, a really close friendship, had become more and more attractive.

It was embarrassing, that's what it was. She was a thirty-two-year-old woman, for heaven's sake, and she was having a bit of a *crush* on someone? She'd actually felt herself blushing when she'd gone into the locker room this morning and had seen him for real again and not just in a rather crumpled photograph. And Felicity Wilson *never* blushed. She needed to get a grip and keep any interaction between herself and this new team member strictly, and utterly, professional until she could get her head around this.

It was just so different.

Not that Fizz was a stranger to interactions with men. She'd experienced a wide spectrum, in fact— from having been head over heels in love at one point in her life to having to fight off determined advances from extremely undesirable people at the other end of the spectrum—but *this* was different.

She wasn't in any danger of falling in love, of course. That state of mind—which was pretty close to being crazy, given how it could take over your life— had been a one-off and had died at the same time that Hamish had. Any relationship in the years since that life-changing event had…well, it had just happened. Had come from a friendship that involved doing things together, preferably extreme sports, and sex just became part of the friendship. A bonus that got added in later, when and if it seemed like a good idea.

That was why she was feeling so flustered right now, wasn't it? Because she wasn't even friends with Cooper Sinclair yet but she was already thinking about how nice it would be to touch him? To *be* touched?

She needed to take a big step back. Fast. It had to be Cooper who took that first step towards friendship. Chasing men—like falling in love—was another thing that Fizz never did, but she'd given off some pretty strong signals already, hadn't she? Like voicing her approval of Cooper's statement that he had no intention of having kids by letting him know that she felt the same way. Had he sensed the underlying message that a friendship between them could work well because neither of them was interested in something long term or permanent? That neither of them would be harbouring secret plans for a potential future?

The eggs arrived, on thick pieces of buttered, sourdough toast, sprinkled with fresh parsley.

'Wow...' Cooper eyed his plate after thanking Shirley. 'This looks amazing.' He glanced sideways at Fizz. 'I've never come across an ambulance station or rescue base that has its own cook before.'

'Shirley isn't employed here,' Fizz told him. 'She's a volunteer. Everybody puts into a kitty for a grocery fund.' She ate the first bites of her breakfast in silence but then spoke again. This was good. Just a friendly sort of conversation.

'She's a bit of a legend is our Shirley. Her son's life got saved by a helicopter crew years and years ago and she wanted to thank people so she started baking cakes and bringing them in for morning tea, and organising fundraisers and so on.' She lowered her voice, although Shirley was now stacking dishes into the dishwasher and the clatter meant that she couldn't possibly know she was being talked about.

'After her husband died a few years ago, her involvement here just grew. She started being here in the mornings to cook breakfasts and now she does a roast dinner on a Sunday. I've only been lucky enough to be on a Sunday duty a couple of times but I can tell you that Shirley does the best roast beef and Yorkshire puddings you're likely to get outside England.'

Fizz turned her attention back to her plate but she could feel Cooper's gaze on her face. A thoughtful kind of gaze. Good grief…he could just *look* at her and it felt like a physical touch? This was definitely odd.

'Is that typical of people in this country? That kind of generosity?'

'Well, Shirley's one in a million, of course, but I think it is true to some extent,' she told him. 'And I think that we get to see it more than others in this job. The ambulance service or first response in isolated areas is always run by volunteers who give up a lot of their own time for training and being on duty. I can't count the number of times I've arrived on scene on a callout to find local people going above and beyond to do what they can to help. It's part of what I love about doing this—why I signed up to volunteer.'

'You don't get paid to be here?' Cooper sounded surprised.

'It's one of my hobbies,' Fizz told him. The admiration she caught in his expression was more than a little disconcerting. Okay, she wanted him to be interested in her as a friend but as an equal, not someone on a some sort of pedestal. Finding it so hard to break that eye contact was even worse. How could something become so intense within the space of a single heartbeat? Somehow, she needed to lighten the atmosphere.

'I get a free uniform.' She managed a smile as she dragged her gaze free. 'And great breakfasts. And sometimes cake for morning tea as well.' She wiped up the last of her egg yolk with a crust of the bread and then jumped to her feet, picking up her plate, as her gaze scanned the other people scattered throughout this space. She raised her voice slightly.

'Where do you want me today, Don?'

'You're crewing with Maggie. Aratika One. We'll send you out for anything that's called in as status one. I might send Cooper out with you as third crew if he's on base—if that's okay with you. He's still getting up to speed with all our protocols.'

'Sure.' Fizz nodded, letting Shirley take her plate from her hands. Smiled, even, although her heart had just sunk a little.

She didn't want to work with Cooper Sinclair.

No, that wasn't true. She did want to work with him, she just didn't want him to know that he was messing with her head more than a little. How mortifying would it be if he guessed how often she'd thought about him since their little adventure on the beach? More than that, it was disturbing that she was feeling this way. She didn't want to be hoping for something that might or might not happen. Fizz needed things to be normal. If something happened, great. If it didn't, it didn't matter. It was when you started hoping, or worse—planning, that you left yourself vulnerable to disappointment. Heartbreak, even.

Maybe even a friendship with this man wasn't a good idea.

A friendship with 'benefits' was absolutely not a good idea.

'He needs to go on the next job that involves the

coastguard, too,' Don added. He turned towards Cooper. 'You haven't met anybody there yet, have you?'

'No.' Cooper was taking his empty plate to where Shirley was still busy clearing up.

'Come with me. I've got a copy of their standard operating procedures in my office. You might want to have a browse if you get any downtime today. You've done a training course for boat rescues, though, haven't you?'

'Yes. I did a holiday season with a coastguard unit in Cornwall a few years back.'

Fizz watched the two men head for the stairs. Hopefully, there wouldn't be much in the way of downtime today. The sooner she had the distraction of being whisked away to assist on a job where somebody was critically injured or ill, the better. It wouldn't matter if Cooper was there, either. Once she was focused on a patient, there was no way she would have any head space for anything other than what needed to be done to save a life or at least make someone a lot more comfortable.

She jumped as she heard Shirley's voice right behind her.

'Oh my,' the older woman said. 'He's a bit of a looker, our new lad, isn't he?'

'Oh?' Fizz feigned surprise. 'I hadn't noticed.'

Shirley's breath came out in snort that said she didn't believe a word but she bent to start wiping the table. 'I wonder if he's got a kilt,' she murmured. 'Imagine that…'

'I'd rather not.' Fizz didn't have to feign the sincerity in her voice. Her fingers felt for the pager clipped to her belt, tapping it gently. Willing it to start beeping and advertise an incoming call. With a bit of luck, it would happen very soon, so she'd be out of the building by the time Cooper came back down those stairs.

It was hard to concentrate on the standard operating procedures of the coastguard that related to the safety of extra personnel on board.

Cooper was too aware that Fizz was present in the staffroom as well. Right at the far end of this large space, mind you, because she was having a game of pool with Andy the pilot as they waited for a call to come in, but he was still aware of her.

What had it been about, the intensity in the look she'd given him, just before she'd hurriedly finished her breakfast and almost jumped to her feet to get away from the table? It was confusing, that's what it was.

She'd barely been able to remember his name when she'd seen him again and then she'd given him a look that had made him feel like there was some sort of deep, significant connection between them.

Cooper might not believe in that nonsense about 'love at first sight' but he certainly knew that 'lust at first sight' existed. This didn't feel like a simple mutual sexual attraction, though—he was quite familiar with what that felt like. This felt...different. Unpredictable, perhaps. A bit wild. Dangerous, even...

Rather like Fizz herself.

The first call that came in was for someone to be first on the scene at a traffic accident on the main road that led into Wellington from the north. Joe and Cooper got dispatched and fought their way through the stalled traffic to find a car that had been clipped by a truck and had then gone into the path of another car

in the neighbouring lane. The truck driver was unin-
jured and angry that someone had cut in in front of
him like that.

'I had nowhere to go. You can't just stop a ten-ton
truck like it's a dodgem car, you know?'

The driver and passenger of the third vehicle involved had only minor injuries—a bumped elbow and
a mild whiplash that would need checking out at an
emergency department. The driver of the other car
was still trapped in his vehicle but he was conscious
and said he felt fine. He also smelt strongly of alcohol.

At this time of the morning? Cooper and Joe shared
a glance.

'Must have been a good night out,' Joe murmured.
'Let's see if we can get a collar on him. Once an ambulance gets here, I think we can make ourselves
available again. There's nothing that's going to need
advanced management here and it's going to take a
while.'

A fire service truck had managed to get through the
traffic jam with the help of the police and its crew were
getting their cutting gear ready to free the trapped
driver. Traffic on the other side of the road seemed
to have come to a standstill as well and there were
horns being sounded by frustrated commuters who
just wanted to get to work.

Despite the noise around him, Cooper could still
hear the chop of rotors overhead and looked up to see
one of Aratika's bright yellow rescue helicopters airborne and rapidly gaining height. Was Fizz on board
this time—being taken away to help with a serious
emergency?

Joe noticed the direction of his glance. 'Don't

worry, mate. I'm sure you'll get the chance to go and play later. Fizz is the biggest trauma magnet we've got. It's just a matter of getting your timing right.'

A blip on a nearby siren had cars edging sideways and an ambulance managed to get close enough to the scene to allow its crew to start unloading their gear. Before long Cooper and Joe would be free to make their skills available where they might be really needed.

Cooper smiled. 'As they say…timing is everything.'

And perhaps fate was giving him a chance to take a good look at this instant attraction. To think about it and realise that it really wasn't a very good idea to go any further down that particular track. Fizz was like no other woman he'd ever met and it was quite possible that he could get chewed up and spat out without even seeing it coming.

Due to the crumpled, jammed doors on the driver's side, Cooper had to climb into the other side of the car, the moulded, plastic cervical collar in his hands. He needed to put this on to protect the driver's neck until it could be cleared from injuries, because a crash that had mangled this car enough to trap him had also had a real potential to cause a neck injury. The fact that this patient was drunk meant that he might not be so aware of any warning signs, like pain.

'Don't need that thing,' he told Cooper. 'I'm fine, man…'

'It's just to be on the safe side,' Cooper said. 'Especially for when we get you out of here. Keep as still as you can. I know it's not the most comfortable thing, but it'll keep your neck safe. I'm going to sit behind you while they cut the car up and hold your head to be extra sure it doesn't move, okay?'

The firies covered both Cooper and the driver with a sheet of plastic to protect them from shattering glass as they cut into the mangled metal and then peeled it away to give access to the patient.

The noise of the pneumatic gear was far too loud to be able to talk, or even think particularly coherently for a minute or two. It was a small space of time in which Cooper focused on keeping this patient's neck as safe as possible. And, just for a moment, it occurred to him that he should really keep his *own* neck safe as well. Not physically, but emotionally.

Fizz could be a challenge he might regret going anywhere near.

But Cooper could feel a smile tugging at one corner of his mouth.

That was precisely why he'd come to the other side of the world, wasn't it? For a new challenge?

CHAPTER FOUR

IT WAS ONLY a glance.

It only lasted a split second.

But it was…annoying.

Fizz finally latched the central buckle of her harness together as the skids of the helicopter lifted off the ground. And, yes, she should have had it fastened a few seconds prior to that but she'd been leaning to pull a pair of gloves free from their box so that she could put them on in transit and be ready to hit the ground running at the other end of this short flight.

It wasn't that Cooper had said anything. Or even caught her gaze. But she had seen the tilt of his head and just knew that he was watching. Waiting for her to buckle herself in safely.

Had she really decided that it was a bit disappointing, only minutes ago, that it seemed like she wouldn't even be on base at the same time as Cooper for the whole of her shift today? That she'd have to wait a whole week to see him again, unless she was on duty in the ED when he came in with a patient? Now not only was she heading to an emergency with him in the same helicopter, Cooper was her partner instead of third crew. Maggie had cracked a tooth this afternoon and made an appointment with her dentist for when the shift ended but this job had meant that she might not get back in time. It had been Don's suggestion that Cooper take her place.

'You reckon he's up to speed, Joe?' he'd asked, out of Cooper's earshot.

'I reckon.' Joe had nodded. 'Give him a go. I'm willing to bet he'll cope with anything you can throw at him.'

So here he was. Sitting in seat beside her in the cabin of this helicopter. Being the safety-belt police.

'Did the whole page come through for you, Cooper?' Fizz knew her tone was a little too crisp. 'You up to date on what we're going to?'

'Car through a shop window.' He nodded. He was pulling on a pair of sterile gloves himself. 'Victim hit by the car and then pinned under shelving that came down. Crew on scene are calling for backup for a possible pelvic fracture.'

Fizz nodded. 'If it is a pelvic fracture it could be a time-critical injury and land transport would take far too long with this being rush hour.'

Cooper's head was tilted as he peered down through the window. 'We're heading north, yes?'

'Yes.'

'The road certainly looks crowded.'

'We're heading for Upper Hutt,' Fizz told him. 'One of the four cities that make up Wellington's metropolitan area. The main road north hugs the coast. This one goes inland.'

'There's a lot of forest down there.'

'That's Rimutaka Hill in that direction.' Fizz leaned into her safety harness, stretching towards Cooper to point through the window on his side. 'Beyond that is the Tararua Forest Park. Brilliant for tramping if you're into that kind of thing.'

'Love it.' Cooper nodded. 'How 'bout you?'

Fizz couldn't help her lips curving into a grin. 'I got winched down once in a rescue. It was brilliant.'

Cooper's eyebrows rose. 'You're winch trained?'

'Not exactly. I'm hoping to be before too long, but that time I got taken down in a nappy harness. The patient had a major chest injury that needed a bit of surgery.'

Suddenly, Fizz had to look away from Cooper. Because she was remembering the kind of intimate body contact that was involved when you were strapped to someone else like that. Imagining how different it might have been if Cooper had been the paramedic taking her on that exciting descent into a small clearing in the forest. The thought was gone as soon as it came, but it was enough to ring an alarm bell. Just how had she lost her focus to that extent? A momentary loss of control, maybe, but it was a reminder of why it was disturbing to be experiencing this crush or whatever it was. Her brain hadn't been hijacked by that kind of detour since…well, since she'd fallen in love with Hamish, probably.

It couldn't be allowed to happen again.

'Andy? Have we got any update from the scene?'

'Fire service are still working to stabilise a wall that's been damaged. No update on patient status. We're going to land on a football field that's about two hundred metres from the scene. ETA two minutes.'

Fizz gave a single nod, drawing in a deep breath. Focus was not an issue now. Someone could bleed out internally from a pelvic fracture if one of the main blood vessels had been damaged and the ambulance road crew that had responded to the incident would not have the skills or gear to deal with that kind of critical emergency. She had her harness unfastened the moment the skids were on solid ground again. She shoved one trauma pack towards Cooper and then grabbed a second one herself. She was moving fast, even as she looped the straps over her arms, and she was jogging by the time she spotted a police officer signalling from the edge of the field, but she knew that Cooper was keeping up with her pace. She could feel the solid shape of him so close behind that she would be able to see him if she turned her head just a little.

She didn't. Fizz kept her gaze firmly on where she was heading.

Man, this felt good.

The police officer leading the way to the scene was shouting information over his shoulder as they ran.

'Victim's a fifty-six-year-old male. He was in the direct line of the car when it came through the window at speed. Elderly driver apparently stood on the accelerator instead of the brake.'

'Is he conscious?'

'No. But the paramedics there don't seem to think he's got a head injury. His legs are in a bad way.'

'How far now?'

'Just around this corner. You'll see the crowd.'

Cooper could already see the reflection of flashing lights in the windows of buildings they were passing. He could feel the tension that was always there when you were approaching an emergency situation. There was nothing like this moment in time to make him feel so focused. His brain could work faster, his senses were all on high alert and he had enough experience to be confident that he could deal with whatever was waiting for them.

Them...

This wasn't just about being on the periphery of the action in this new job while he got himself up to speed on any protocols that were a little different from what Cooper was used to and to allow his colleagues to get to know and trust his abilities.

He was the paramedic partner to the doctor on duty right now. Another set of hands, skills and knowledge to complement those of the more highly trained medic. A vital member of this small team. And it *felt* like a team. Maybe it was because they had worked together once already, at that accident scene, but it felt like more than that. It felt like the most natural thing in the world to be loping along beside this woman, heading for what could be a challenging emergency situation. There was a sense of connection—a kind of recognition—that might be disconcerting on a personal level but it was exciting on a professional one. Cooper knew that Fizz would tackle anything. And that she was skilled enough to improve their odds of being successful.

Not only would she tackle anything, mind you, she'd head straight in without giving her own safety enough thought. Cooper actually grabbed her arm as a group of emergency service personnel stepped aside to let them onto the scene.

'Watch out,' he said. 'There's glass everywhere.'

There was. The car had gone through a plate-glass

window and shards of it were still clinging to parts of the frame, looking like the points of vicious spears.

Fizz yanked her arm free. Or maybe she was just continuing to move forward and was too focused on what lay ahead to bother acknowledging the warning. They were beside the car that had crashed into this building now. Cooper could see the backs of people crouched over someone on the floor. He could see broken shelving that had been lifted clear and pieces of timber that were propping up a damaged wall. He could also see the hazards like tins of canned food that were rolling around when they got knocked and wet patches on the floor from broken bottles of liquid. He still had his arm out when Fizz slipped a little on a wet patch but she clearly didn't need, or want, any assistance with her balance this time.

Fair enough, but that wasn't going to stop Cooper keeping an eye out for any other hazards. Or doing whatever he could to mitigate them.

The local ambulance crew looked relieved to have backup. They relayed all the information they had as Fizz and Cooper smoothly took over the management of what was clearly a critically injured patient and they were there to assist as much as they could. Fire officers were working around them to try and clear debris and make sure the area they were working in was stable, providing background noise to the urgent communication taking place between the members of the medical team.

'Blood pressure's dropping…systolic's down to ninety-five.'

'I'd like another line in. We're going to need a blood transfusion.'

'Multiple fractures to both legs…'

'I can't get a femoral pulse…'

'Pelvis is unstable. Let's get a pelvic binder on…'

'Cooper? I want to get control of his airway. Can you draw up some drugs for me, please? For an RSI?'

'Sure.' Cooper unrolled the kit to find, draw up and then administer the anaesthetic agents required for the rapid sequence intubation. He was right beside Fizz, his fingers on the neck of their patient to provide cricoid pressure as she carefully inserted the laryngoscope into the mouth and then tilted it until she had a clear view. He had the bougie ready to put in her hand and then the tube to slip over the top for her to position in the trachea. And then it was time to pull the guide device out.

'I have the bougie—do you have the tube?'

'I have the tube.'

Cooper attached the bag mask and delivered a breath as Fizz unhooked her stethoscope from around her neck to check the correct placement of the breathing tube by listening to lung sounds. She looked up and gave a single, satisfied nod as he handed the bag mask to one of the paramedics to keep up the ventilations.

'All good,' she said.

An understatement, Cooper decided. That whole, intense procedure had been completed in no more than about thirty seconds. And that was partly because they had worked together so well.

It wasn't just their physical skills that meshed so well, either. Cooper got the impression that Fizz felt the same kind of connection and confidence in him that he did in her—that sense of recognition—as if they already knew each other?

'I can't get a femoral pulse,' Fizz said a moment later as she checked their patient again. 'Have you got a BP?'

'Still dropping. Unreadable.'

'He's got a significant haemorrhage going on. You familiar with the REBOA procedure, Coop?'

Some distant part of his brain registered the fact that she'd shortened his name—as if she knew him so well he needed a nickname—but it didn't shift his focus.

'The insertion of the balloon catheter to occlude the aorta and stop internal haemorrhage?'

'Yep.'

'I've read about it. Seen video. It's not something that was part of our protocols.'

'There's not many places that do it.'

Fizz caught his gaze and held it for a moment, a query in her eyes. He knew she was asking if he felt comfortable assisting her in what would be an advanced invasive procedure. His single nod was subtle but sufficient.

'We'll give him another unit of blood, but if his pressure doesn't come up, I think that's our next step.'

It was Cooper who took the next set of vital signs as the second unit of blood was pushed as fast as possible by someone squeezing the bag with both hands.

'Systolic of eighty-five,' he reported.

It looked like Fizz let out a breath she'd been holding. 'Okay...let's get going. The sooner we can get him to Theatre the better. Can we get a stretcher in here, please?'

With so many people available it was a quick task to package their patient on the stretcher and then carry him back to the helicopter. As the clamshell doors closed on the cabin and they took off, Cooper checked his watch to realise that they'd been on the ground for less than twenty minutes. They would have this critically injured person in the emergency department—maybe even in an operating theatre—well within the golden hour of dealing with major trauma.

He'd been impressed with Felicity Wilson the first time he'd seen her in action but right now he was blown away. It had been a privilege to work with her and he couldn't wait to do it again. On a professional level, he had never worked with anyone that made him feel part of such a tight team and facing future challenges together was an exciting prospect.

It was another incentive to keep their relationship solely professional. This was an opportunity to work with someone who could push his professional boundaries and help him improve his skills and knowledge. Who would be stupid enough to risk that by acting on an attraction that could potentially wreck what held the promise of being an extraordinary working relationship?

'He's good.' Fizz had dropped into Don's office when they'd finally got back to base. 'I'm happy to work with him as double crew any time and I'm sure any other HEMS doctor would agree.'

'Good to know.' Don nodded. He closed his laptop and slid it into a bag. 'High time I headed home. I was just waiting to hear how the job went.'

'It was a good challenge. We almost got to do a REBOA procedure for haemorrhagic shock.'

'Wow...that doesn't happen often.'

'It was probably a good thing for our patient that it didn't need to happen today. Having the capability to carry blood products with us made the difference there.' Fizz was following Don down the stairs. She could hear the murmur of voices in the staffroom and wondered if Cooper was still here.

She hadn't been entirely truthful in the assessment she'd given the base manager about Cooper's performance. He wasn't simply 'good' at his job. He was... well, he was something special. Fizz couldn't think of anyone else she had ever worked with where it felt like half the communication was almost telepathic. Like that rapid sequence intubation. Whatever she had needed had been available without having to ask for it—as if she'd had an extra pair of her own hands, or that they'd been working as a team for years and years.

It almost made up for that annoying streak of taking responsibility for her safety, like the way he'd tried to steer her away from the broken glass she had been quite well aware of. She didn't need to be protected. Didn't *want* to be...

Except that, deep down, it was rather nice to have someone looking out for her, wasn't it?

As if they cared? Or was it because Cooper thought she was feminine and therefore fragile? That was why it was so annoying, of course, but it was disturbing at the same time, because this Scotsman was big enough to make Fizz *feel* feminine and, if she was honest with herself, she kind of liked that as well.

He was still in the staffroom. The night shift crew members he had been talking to responded to a callout as Fizz entered, however, and Don headed home, after telling Cooper he was going to take him off being in a third crew, supervised position on the team.

'You've had the tick of approval from both Fizz and Joe,' Don told him. 'And I know how high their standards are.'

Cooper grinned at Fizz as they found themselves alone in the room. 'Thanks,' he said.

'What for?' Oh, man... She was going to have to get used to that smile but it wasn't going to be easy. It did something really weird to the pit of her stomach.

'Giving me a tick.'

'You earned it.' Fizz glanced at her watch. 'What are you still doing here? You should have clocked off an hour ago.'

'So should you.'

'I was finishing up my paperwork. It's been a busy day.'

'And I was restocking the kits. It was a good chance to get properly familiar with the storeroom and Danny was happy to stay on for a while and help. He's a nice guy.'

'Mmm. Weren't you going to see that room in Maggie's house this evening?'

Cooper looked surprised that she'd remembered. 'I had a text from her, asking if we could put it off until tomorrow. She got held up at the dentist.'

'Hope her mouth isn't too sore. Which reminds me... I'm starving...' Fizz headed towards the bench and the large biscuit tin that lived in one corner. 'I wonder if any of Shirley's cookies are left.' She prised the lid off the tin. 'Ooh...even better—it's cake... Carrot cake, my favourite...' She turned her head as she opened a drawer and reached for a knife. 'Want a piece, Coop? *Ow…*'

The sound had Cooper on his feet in a split second. 'What is it?'

'Nothing.' Fizz ripped a paper towel from the nearby roll. 'I just nicked my thumb.'

'Let me see…' Cooper was right beside her now, holding out his hand.

'No…it's just a little nick. It's nothing.'

Except the blood was soaking through the paper towel. She needed another one. Cooper was ripping one off the roll and folding it into a small square.

'You need to put some pressure on it.'

'I *know* that.' Fizz gave him a withering glance. 'I did go to medical school, you know.'

He had one hand circling hers, the other waiting with his pressure pad for her to give him access to her injured thumb. Dammit…he wasn't going to give up, was he? She didn't want someone caring about her like this. Looking out for her to make sure she was safe and jumping in to take care of her if she was injured. *Protecting* her…

It could be that Cooper was taking the first step towards a relationship that was more than simply professional. Towards a friendship that she already knew she would welcome. She had decided, only this morning, that she would step back and wait for him to make that first move—because she wanted it *too* much?

But…this was weirdly nerve-racking. Scary, even.

Because Fizz knew that the attraction she felt for this man was not due to having been single for so long. Or that they'd met each other by sharing a dramatic incident. She recognised, on more than one level now, that Cooper Sinclair was special. That there was something between them that was very different from anything she had ever experienced before—even with the man she had chosen to marry.

Her nerves made it easy to back away from that attraction. To tap, instead, into the annoyance of having someone treat her as if she was in need of protection.

'I'm a big girl, Cooper,' she snapped. 'I can look after myself. I don't need you telling me to watch out for anything. Or watch me to make sure I put a safety belt on. I don't need you to look after my damn thumb, either. If I'm stupid enough to do something careless, I'm quite capable of dealing with the consequences.'

His gaze was steady. He didn't look at all put out by her snapping at him. 'I know that,' he said quietly. 'But we're part of a team, Fizz, and team members look out for each other. It's not a weakness to let other people help, you know. And, yeah…maybe I go overboard a bit sometimes but that's just the way I am. I…ah…lost someone once and it wouldn't have happened if there'd been a bit more attention to some basic safety. I'm not about to let it happen again but it's no reflection on how capable I know you are, believe me.'

There was something about that sincere tone of his voice that was making it difficult to keep hold of that annoyance. Or perhaps it was what he was saying—that the death of someone he'd worked with had affected him deeply because he'd cared about his colleague that much? She had sensed that he was a nice person from the first moment she'd met him. Big. Solid. Totally dependable. The kind of person you'd be lucky to work with or have as a friend.

Or maybe it was more to do with that steady gaze

from eyes that she hadn't looked at this closely before. Hazel eyes, with a warmth to their golden brown that made her think of…good grief…teddy bears? Yes… she could swear that she'd had a beloved bear when she was very young that had had eyes of exactly that colour. She'd gone to sleep cuddling that bear every night for many years…

Somehow, that awareness of the colour of Cooper's eyes had made her let her guard down. He had gently pushed her hand away, had a look at the cut on her thumb and was now applying pressure to the wound himself.

'It might take a few minutes,' he murmured. 'It's quite deep but I don't think it needs a stitch. We just need to stop it bleeding.'

'Mmm…' The sound was a little strangled. Fizz stared down at her thumb because she didn't dare look up at Cooper again. She hadn't been this aware of the sheer size of him since he'd been holding her hand that day they'd first met, to help her keep her balance on those rocks. It was something deeper than being made to feel feminine, wasn't it? It was almost as if there was a much younger Fizz still inside. A child who cuddled teddy bears when she went to sleep. Who needed her hand held sometimes.

It actually brought a lump to her throat, along with a swirl of something like confusion. Fear, almost…and that was enough for her gaze to flick upwards again. What was it about this man that was so different?

She found that same steady gaze on her own.

'Almost there,' he said softly. 'Another thirty seconds or so should do it.'

Fizz knew she should break that eye contact. She

should also pull her hand away from his and look after her injury herself but she did neither of those things and that was undoing.

She couldn't move. She couldn't look away. She was powerless against the strength of a pull she'd never felt before. An attraction so fierce that what she wanted right now—the *only* thing she wanted right now— was for Cooper Sinclair to bend his head and kiss her.

Was she willing it to happen? Was that why she could see the way his eyes darkened as he seemed to catch her unspoken desire and reflect it back at her? Why his head started to drift down?

He seemed to catch himself with a jerk. It was Cooper who broke the eye contact. Fizz could feel him carefully peeling the wad of paper towel from her thumb. When he spoke, his voice was a little raw.

'I think it's stopped,' he told her. 'We're all good.'

Fizz nodded as she stepped back. 'I'll go and find a plaster,' she said.

Her voice sounded a little odd as well. Shaky, almost, and she knew why. Cooper had got it wrong, hadn't he?

It hadn't stopped.

Whatever it was between them was just getting started and Fizz had the feeling that, if it went any further, it would be a lot harder to stop than any blood loss from a small cut.

She would be playing with fire to give in to this attraction. This was the second time today that she'd had a momentary loss of control, even though she'd thought she'd taken heed of the warning the first time. If it was this hard to fight the pull towards this man when they barely knew each other, how hard would it be to control if it got unleashed?

The thought was a little terrifying.

But it was also more than a little exciting.

It wasn't a physically dangerous situation but, oddly, it seemed to offer the promise of just as much of an adrenaline rush.

And Felicity Wilson knew only too well that she had a little bit of an issue with seeking out the thrill that came with the release of that particular hormone. She had it more under control these days, mind you. She'd harnessed it, to enhance her life instead of using it to escape things that had threatened to destroy her life.

This crush, or attraction, or whatever it was, was simply the rush of a different variety of hormones, wasn't it? It was purely physical. She wasn't falling in love with this man. For heaven's sake…this was only the second time she'd seen him. She'd been dating Hamish for half their time at medical school before they had both realised how much in love in they were.

Fizz put two plasters on her thumb just to be on the safe side. As she reached to put the small first-aid kit back on top of the fridge, she slid a sideways glance at Cooper. He'd cut a slice of the cake and put it on a plate, along with a fork and a neatly folded paper towel as a serviette.

Good grief…he ate cake like he was at an afternoon tea with his grandmother? With a fork? Fizz had never eaten cake with a fork in her life. It didn't fit with her impressions of Cooper's sheer masculinity and it was another dip in what was becoming an emotional roller-coaster.

To be feeling such strong emotions was not normal. Fizz took her friendships with men as they came. If they went further than simply friendship it was great but if they didn't that was no problem. Of course she enjoyed the chemistry of physical attraction and the satisfaction of great sex but she didn't let it take control at a level that could disrupt her life.

She didn't do planning for a future in a relationship or hope that it would become something significant because that was the best protection there was from disappointment or heartbreak. But she had wanted that kiss, hadn't she? She'd been hoping for it enough to consider how exciting it would be to play with fire.

It was confusing, that's what it was. And the best way that Fizz could find to balance that disturbing level of attraction was to try and find something to build a barrier. Something undesirable about Cooper. Like his over-protectiveness. Or the fact that he could do something as prim and proper as eating cake with a fork. That was kind of old-fashioned. Stuffy, even. Right now, Fizz was tempted to go and cut a slice of cake for herself and stuff it into her mouth using nothing more than her hand, right in front of Cooper. To let him know just how stuffy she considered him to be. How strait-laced and old-fashioned. Had she really entertained the idea of a friendship with benefits with him? He probably wouldn't dream of having that kind of casual relationship.

She turned, in fact, to do exactly that with the cake, only to be faced by...by that *smile*... The one that gave him crinkles at the corners of his eyes and made his whole face light up.

'Here you go,' Cooper said, pushing the plate along the bench in her direction. 'Enjoy...'

CHAPTER FIVE

'Fizz… I'm so glad you're still here.'

'Laura…' Fizz was startled to see her friend and workmate in the emergency department of the Royal as she came out of an office, a medical journal that she'd been wanting to read in her hands. 'What on earth are you doing back at work? You finished an hour ago.'

'It's Harrison. I think he's broken his arm.'

'Oh, no…' But Fizz was confused. 'Where is he?'

'Cubicle Three. He's with Cooper. He drove us in. I came looking for you because I was hoping you might be able to see him. You know how he is with strangers—especially men.'

'I know.' Five-year-old Harrison was small for his age and could be easily frightened. 'But he's okay with Cooper?'

'Amazingly so. I was a bit worried when he moved into the house because…well, he's so big, isn't he? But there's something about him, isn't there? And kids pick up on that sort of thing. It's only been a week but you'd think they'd known each other for years. And he'd just got home when Harry fell. He looked after him right from when it happened.'

Fizz pulled back the curtain to Cubicle Three and, for a heartbeat, her breath caught in her chest.

Cooper Sinclair was sitting on the bed. Harrison was sitting on his lap, leaning back into the crook of one of Cooper's arms. It made him look even smaller than Fizz knew the little boy was. It also made him look as if he'd never been so well protected and Fizz could easily imagine exactly how that felt.

She knew what it was like to have this big man looking after you. Not that she'd seen Cooper since last week, when he'd insisted on taking care of her cut thumb. Part of her had been hoping she'd see him in the emergency department—part of her had been relieved that she hadn't. She'd known what it would be like to make eye contact with Cooper again. How potentially awkward it could be if they were both thinking about the same thing. Sure enough, even the briefest contact as her gaze dropped straight from the man to the child in his arms was enough to confirm she'd been right. Laura had no idea how correct she was. There certainly was something about Cooper Sinclair.

It was still hanging there in the air.

The kiss that hadn't happened.

'Hey… Harry… What have you been up to?' Fizz was smiling reassuringly but she was taking in how pale his face was and the way he was holding one arm against his chest. An arm that was buried in a cushion that had been tied around the hand and wrist.

'I fell over,' Harry whispered.

'He was swinging on the gate.' Laura moved around Fizz to stand as close as she could to Cooper. She reached out to stroke Harry's hair. 'It came off its hinge, didn't it, sweetheart? And you fell onto the footpath and hurt your arm.'

'Simple FOOSH,' Cooper added. 'Colles' fracture. We improvised with a pillow splint and then it didn't hurt so much, did it, buddy?'

'Thank goodness Cooper was there,' Laura said. 'It's funny, isn't it? We deal with a lot worse than this in here all the time but when it's your own kid, it's so different.'

'Can I have a peep?' Fizz touched the edge of the cushion protecting the injured arm.

Harrison seemed to shrink back further into Cooper's arms and Laura leaned in give him a kiss and reassure him.

'It's okay… Fizz is the doctor today and she just needs to have a look to see what to do next to fix up your arm.'

'But it's going to hurt…' Harrison was clearly trying hard to be brave but tears were imminent.

'How 'bout I undo the bandage, just a little bit?' Cooper's voice was a gentle rumble. 'Just to let Fizz have a peep.'

'You know Cooper won't hurt you,' Laura added. 'He's looking after you, isn't he?'

Harrison nodded but his lips were wobbling.

Fizz watched Cooper very carefully start to unroll the bandage he'd used to secure the soft cushion around Harrison's wrist. It had been the perfect splint, with the filling of the cushion moulding into the classic dinner fork shape of the Colles' fracture and supporting the arm and hand on either side so it couldn't move any further. Both Cooper and Laura were focused on

Harrison and Fizz could feel…something. Some kind of bond… A trust between the three of them?

Cooper had only been living in the shared house for a week. Surely there couldn't be anything going on between him and Laura already, could there?

It was an unprofessional thing to be thinking about right now. Even more unprofessional was the flash of something like envy that came as an afterthought. Jealousy, even? No…but maybe regret that she'd let an opportunity disappear. Why on earth had she waited for Cooper to kiss her that night instead of just making it happen herself? What had that been about? She might never find out what it might have been like now.

The thought was gone as instantly as it had arrived. If Cooper had wanted to kiss her, he would have. She was not about to chase someone who wasn't interested. Or chase anyone, for that matter.

'Can you wiggle your fingers for me, Harry?' she asked.

'No.'

'Did you try, buddy?' Cooper was stifling a smile. He held out a giant hand so that it was side by side with Harrison's tiny one. 'Like this…' He wiggled those long fingers slowly, as though he was playing an imaginary piano.

Oh, help… Fizz could actually feel the tingle on her own skin, as if those fingers were touching it. This was getting ridiculous.

But Harrison was moving *his* fingers now. And his thumb, which was enough to reassure Fizz that his median nerve hadn't been damaged. The colour of his hand was good, too, so there were unlikely to be any major complications from this fracture.

'We need to take an X-ray of your arm, Harry,' she told him. 'It's a special photo of the bones inside it. And then we're going to put a cast on it, which is like a hard sleeve and it will stop your arm moving so it can get better.'

'I know what a cast is. Sally at school had one. It was pink.'

'Do you want a pink one?'

'No…pink is for girls.'

'Not necessarily,' Fizz said firmly. 'If you want pink then that's cool. It won't be a coloured one for a few days, though. We put a big, white one on first because your wrist is quite swollen and it needs time for that to go down. Now, how 'bout you and Cooper here have a chat about what colour it's going to be later on, while I have a talk to Mummy for a minute before you go up to X-ray? Is that okay?'

Both Harrison and Cooper nodded. Laura followed Fizz through the curtains.

'We'll get the X-ray and, if it's a straightforward fracture, we'll realign it and get a cast on in no time.'

'Pain relief?'

'Did you give him any paracetamol?'

'Yes…after Cooper suggested it. Honestly, my brain turned to mush.'

'I think we'll use some intranasal fentanyl for the realignment. It's fast acting, lasts long enough and you'll only have to wait another thirty minutes or so afterwards before you can take him home.'

'That's a relief. Poor Cooper's not getting much of a free evening. I don't like imposing on him but Maggie and Jack were both out.'

'He looks happy enough.'

'And he's so good with Harry. I can't believe how lucky we are to have got him as a flatmate.' Laura's eyebrows rose as she took in the expression on Fizz's face. 'What?'

'Nothing… I was just thinking about how good he is with Harry.'

If Fizz was honest, she was really thinking about what he'd be like as a partner. As a father, even.

He'd be perfect, probably.

Every woman's dream. Every woman other than herself, that is. Someone like Laura, perhaps?

Laura was still staring at her and comprehension flooded her face. 'Oh, no…it's *nothing* like that… Good grief, Fizz. How could you even think of something like that? Not in a million years…'

Fizz's smile was apologetic. She knew that Laura's relationship with Harrison's father had been traumatic enough to have made her shy away from any relationships with men.

'I have no idea.' She sighed. 'Ignore me. It's just that…like you said, there's something about him…'

Laura's expression had changed. A corner of her mouth curved upwards. '*You* like him, don't you, Fizz?'

Fizz shook her head. 'Not like that. Any more than you do. Now…let's get this show on the road, shall we? If Cooper's happy to stay, he could carry Harry up to X-ray, otherwise let's find a wheelchair. The sooner we get onto it, the sooner we can all get home.'

There was no question of abandoning Laura and Harrison in the emergency department, even though Cooper knew they would be extremely well looked after.

They even had a personal physician who was a family friend. It had been evident from the moment he'd come in here with the child in his arms that Harrison was nervous of strangers so it was amazing that he'd accepted *him* into his life so willingly over the last week.

It felt like a privilege to be trusted more than other people and Cooper wasn't about to break that trust by leaving his new flatmate and her kid here by themselves. So he carried Harrison to X-ray and back to the fracture clinic and he helped Laura reassure him that it would be no time at all until his arm was comfy in its new cast. The pain relief was effective and the procedure to straighten the small arm was straightforward, and then it was just a matter of observing him until the cast had dried enough to be solid and for the sedation to wear off.

'You stayed late for us,' Laura said to Fizz. 'Thank you so much.'

'It was my pleasure.'

'And you gave up half your evening,' she said to Cooper. 'I can't thank you enough.'

'It was no problem.'

'You must be starving. How 'bout I cook something when we get home? For you, too, Fizz. I owe you both.'

'You don't want to be cooking,' Fizz said firmly. 'Harrison's going to need all your attention when you get home and you'll be wanting to get him settled. I'll bet you're exhausted after all this.'

'But…'

'I'll drive you home,' Cooper offered. 'We could pick up some takeout food on the way.'

Laura looked at Cooper and then at Fizz, her expression thoughtful. 'I've got a better idea,' she said.

'I'll drive myself and Harry home and you two can go and get some dinner. My treat.'

'Oh, no… I'm sure Cooper's got better things to do with the rest of his evening.'

Fizz was giving Laura an odd look and, for a moment, Cooper was bemused. Was there something going on here that he wasn't privy to? The way Fizz was avoiding his gaze and looking slightly flustered reminded him of when he'd seen her in the locker room at the base the first day they had been there together. When he had thought it interesting that his presence seemed to be unsettling for her for some reason.

That thought morphed instantly into remembering the end of that day. When he'd been putting pressure on that cut on her thumb. When he'd come within a heartbeat of kissing her. He could have sworn that she'd wanted him to but something didn't quite fit. It just seemed out of character for this strong, confident woman, in the same way that being flustered seemed unlikely. If Felicity Wilson wanted to be kissed, Cooper was quite sure that she was more than capable of initiating that herself. He also had the impression that a simple kiss would not be enough for someone who thrived on the thrill of adventure. She would probably want more. A lot more.

That thought was enough to send a spear of sensation through Cooper's body and drive most coherent thought away. He knew this was probably not sensible but there was an opportunity here, if he was game enough to throw caution to the wind and take it.

'Actually, I don't,' he found himself saying aloud. 'I'd love to get some dinner and I'm sure you know the restaurants around here a lot better than I do.'

'Go down the waterfront,' Laura encouraged. 'There's lots of awesome places and it's not far to walk from here.'

Fizz caught Cooper's gaze, finally, and it looked like she was trying to decide whether to accept some kind of challenge.

He could understand that. For himself, this felt like he was holding a match and contemplating striking it against the side of the box but knowing, at the same time, that this particular match had the ability to self-ignite. Also knowing that the ensuing conflagration held the possibility of getting dangerously out of control.

The eye contact went on for a split second too long. Long enough for Cooper to know they were both thinking of the same thing.

That almost kiss...

He saw the movement of Fizz's throat as she swallowed. Then her chin tilted as if she was confident of coping with whatever challenge she might choose to take and one corner of her mouth curved into a half-smile.

'I *am* starving,' she said. 'And I could show you one of my favourite restaurants if you like pub grub, Coop.'

'My all-time favourite.'

The smile widened. 'Give me five minutes. I'll just get changed out of my scrubs.'

Five minutes was enough to carry a still drowsy Harrison back to Laura's car and strap him into his car seat.

'You sure you don't want me to come with you?'

'I'm sure. Go and have a lovely dinner with Fizz.'

Laura reached into her shoulder bag and pulled out her wallet but Cooper shook his head.

'Don't be daft. You're not paying for my dinner.'

'It's just to say thank you.'

'There's no need,' Cooper said firmly. He was smiling as he turned away before Laura could protest any further. Whether she'd intended to or not, his new flatmate had pretty much set him up on a date with Fizz, hadn't she? Maybe it was him who should be thanking her...

Fizz drank beer rather than wine and somehow that didn't surprise Cooper.

She also chose a meal that needed to be eaten without cutlery and would, no doubt, get messy.

Cooper found himself grinning as he ordered the spare ribs as well. This was already more interesting than any date he'd been on in a very long time.

Not that either of them were admitting this was anything more than a meal between colleagues and potential friends, mind you. The conversation as they'd walked from the hospital to the section of the city near the harbourside that was brimming with restaurants, cafés and nightclubs had been no more than the polite sort of 'getting to know someone' queries and responses.

Cooper had told Fizz he'd been born and raised in Edinburgh, had gone to an English university and had never had any ambition to be anything other than a paramedic after he'd given up his small-boy dream of being an astronaut. He had learned that Fizz was a fifth-generation New Zealander and that it was a percentage of Maori and not Mediterranean blood that had given her that amazing olive skin and those dark eyes. She had grown up in a small, rural town not far from Wellington but was now loving her waterfront apartment that was close to this restaurant. She also told him that she had gone to medical school in the south island city of Dunedin, which she said had the reputation of being the most Scottish city in the world outside Scotland.

'You really should visit Dunedin one day,' she said, as she clinked her tall glass of lager against his. They had found a quiet corner in this quirky gastro pub and were perched on stools on either side of a small butcher's block table. 'Especially if you start getting homesick for Edinburgh.'

'I won't get homesick,' he assured her. 'I'm loving being on this side of the world.'

'It's a long way to have come for a new job.' Fizz wiped a streak of foam off her top lip as she gave Cooper a curious glance. 'Why here and not somewhere in Europe or America or Australia, even?' There was a mischievous glint in her eyes. 'Are you running away from an ex-wife?'

'Nope.' Cooper held her gaze. They were moving onto much more personal ground, apparently. 'I just came for the adventure. Never been married. How 'bout you?'

'Yep. I got married.' Her tone was offhand. And then she shrugged. 'Once was enough.'

Cooper's glass of lager stopped halfway between the table and his mouth. He really hadn't expected to hear that. And, to be honest, he was a bit shocked as well. What kind of bastard had she been married to that would make her dismiss the possibility of ever going down that road again?

'How long did it last?' he asked.

'Two days,' Fizz responded.

Cooper's glass hit the table at the same time as his bark of laughter emerged. He opened his mouth to make some quip about not having given it much of a go but then he saw the way Fizz's face had suddenly stilled and he actually felt a chill ripple down his spine.

'Oh, my God…' he said slowly. 'What happened?'

Fizz was silent for another long moment and then she spoke without looking up. 'It was the second day of our honeymoon. We were on an island off Fiji and Hamish decided he was going to try parasailing. Off the back of a jet boat, you know?'

Cooper nodded but said nothing. He was still reeling from realising just how far he'd managed to put his foot in his mouth.

'They hadn't done the harness up properly. I was sitting on the beach and trying to take photographs when he fell. They reckon he broke his neck as he hit the water.'

'I'm so sorry… That's…just horrible.'

'Yeah…' Fizz turned her head. Was she hoping their food would arrive quickly so that she could change the subject? 'Well, ten years is a long time. I learned how to manage alone and I got my life back together.'

'More than back together from what I can see,' Cooper told her. 'I found out that you're a legend amongst the emergency services here even before I got into town properly. And I've seen you in action and I know how good you are at your job.'

'It's everything to me,' Fizz said quietly. 'My career.'

'Me, too.'

The moment of silence between them this time acknowledged a shared passion. A connection. But Cooper could feel the frown on his face and Fizz noticed it at the same time.

'What?'

'You surprise me, that's all.'

'In what way?'

'Having a tragedy like that would make a lot of people more cautious.' Like he had become himself? 'Unless you were even wilder ten years ago than you are now?'

Fizz's lips quirked. 'You think I'm wild?'

'You take risks. I'm not sure that you take enough time to assess how dangerous something is before you decide to do it.'

'I assess. I just do it fast. And in some situations you don't really have a choice. You're talking about me getting those kids out of the car in the surf, aren't you? Would you have stood back when you saw that little girl crying at the window?'

'No…'

'Of course you wouldn't. Oh…that looks like our food arriving.'

A huge platter of barbecued pork ribs went onto the centre of their rustic wooden table flanked by bowls of warm water with lemon slices floating on the top to wash sticky fingers. For several minutes they both concentrated on eating like cavemen, ripping delicious shreds of sauce-drenched, slow-cooked meat off the bones.

'Good, isn't it?' Fizz dropped another bone onto an

empty plate. She sucked some sauce off her fingers before she reached for another rib.

'The best.' Cooper had to drag his gaze away from Fizz licking her fingers. He'd known he was playing with fire, coming out like this with Fizz, and right now he could feel the heat as a solid force. He had to reach for his beer again in the hope of cooling himself off.

'To be honest,' Fizz said, 'I wasn't remotely wild ten years ago. I was a complete nerd. I only met Hamish because we were both nerds who turned up to the study group that got organised the first day we were at med school.'

The mention of the husband she'd lost was more effective in turning down the heat than a gulp of beer. Was the fact that she would never try replacing him the reason that she was never going to get married again? Had she loved him so much she hadn't even embarked on another meaningful relationship in the last ten years? The idea of competing with a ghost for any sort of attention was daunting. Cooper knew how strong a presence a ghost could have and how much they could influence your life.

'I find that hard to believe,' he admitted. 'I get the impression that you're a complete adrenaline junkie.'

'I am.' Fizz nodded. 'And you know whose fault it was that I became one?'

'Whose?'

'Hamish's.'

She'd shocked him again, hadn't she?

Fizz had seen the moment he'd realised that the fact she'd been married for only two days wasn't some kind of joking matter. That it had been a tragedy.

The atmosphere between them had been very casual up to that point. They had simply been two colleagues going out for dinner and it was a good chance to get to know each other better.

Except they both knew there was more to it than that, didn't they? There were undercurrents between them that were strong enough for Laura to have picked up on. Strong enough to have led to her impulsive idea of doing a bit of matchmaking by pushing them together for dinner. And there was a sense of something very different about Cooper that was attracting Fizz even more strongly than it was warning her to stay away.

And here she was, talking about something that she never talked about. To anyone. Something far more personal than the kind of conversation they'd started this evening with. She'd said quite enough already, telling him about her honeymoon tragedy, but it seemed like there was more that Fizz wanted to say. Why? Did she want Cooper to understand why she was the way she was? To take on board the fact that there were reasons why she would never be the kind of person he might be looking for to share his life? Except...he had given the impression that he wasn't looking for someone to settle down with when he'd said he wasn't interested in having his own children. And why else did people go looking for a permanent relationship?

'I was so angry with him,' Fizz said softly. 'We'd had everything so carefully planned, you know? We'd waited until we were through med school and our first junior years before we got married. We were going to wait another five years before we started a family. He was going to be a cardiologist and I was going to go into general practice so I could go part time when the kids were young. And then he went and got himself killed and it felt like someone had taken my life and screwed it up and thrown it away.'

Cooper was nodding slowly. The set of his mouth implied a genuine understanding of what that felt like. The expression in his eyes confirmed that he really did understand and empathise.

'Things were rough for a long time,' Fizz added slowly. 'Really rough…'

His eyes darkened. He knew what that was like, too, didn't he? Not that Fizz wanted this conversation to get any heavier than it already was. Or to think too much about that time herself. Even after all these years and her increasing professional understanding of mental health issues like depression, she could still feel the sense of shame that had dogged her for not being able to pull herself out of that dark space quickly enough. For having to pretend to be the independent, capable person everybody believed she was until it became a reality.

'And then I went away for a weekend,' she added hurriedly. 'And I saw some people parasailing and that tipped me over the edge. I couldn't understand why anyone could be stupid enough to do something like that for pleasure, so you know what I did?'

She could see the movement of Cooper's Adam's apple as he swallowed—as if it wasn't easy.

'You decided to try it yourself?'

Oh…help…

It felt like he knew her so well already. The idea that someone could 'get' her so easily was undeniably powerful. Fizz could feel it sucking her in. Making her say things she would never have confessed to anyone else.

'I didn't care if I died and I was too angry to be scared until my feet left the ground and then I was absolutely terrified. But then it happened.'

'The rush?'

Fizz nodded. 'The rush. For the first time in about a year, I actually felt alive again. As if life really was worth living.'

'So you did it again.'

It wasn't a question. It seemed like Cooper understood more than why she had done something so scary the first time. He would probably understand the rest of it, too. The way she had tapped into that power of being brave and independent to gain confidence that she could look after herself. That she could not only get out of that dark space and find life worth living again but that she could protect herself from ever having to go through something like that again. The idea that someone else could understand that much about what had shaped her life was a bit of a rush all in itself.

'I tried everything,' she confided. 'I think the best ever rush was bungee jumping. Have you ever tried that, Coop?'

He shook his head.

'Did you get that base newsletter this week? Did you notice that there are registration spaces still left for the high country and mountain rescue training weekend in Queenstown in a couple of months' time?'

'Yeah…' Cooper looked puzzled. 'Don suggested I go. I've already done some mountain rescue training in Scotland and he'd like me to extend that so I can do some in-house training for the base. But what's that got to do with bungee jumping?'

'As far as I know, Queenstown is the birthplace of bungee jumping,' Fizz told him. 'The best place, anyway. You could do it while you're down there for the course.'

'Are you kidding?' Cooper looked horrified. 'You could go blind from a retinal detachment doing something like bungee jumping. It's crazy.'

'There's the white-water jet boat rides through rapids, too. Queenstown is like the adventure tourism capital of the world.' Fizz could feel her smile widening. 'And there's a very cool drive into an old gold-mining site that's an adrenaline rush all by itself.' She could feel an impulsive bubble that was about to burst. 'Hey… I could come along, too, and cheer you on. I'd love to do some training in the mountains.'

'Training in the mountains might be good for you. You'd have to learn a lot of safety rules.' But Cooper was smiling.

'A bit of adventure tourism might be good for *you*,' Fizz countered. 'You can die from something totally random that could happen at any moment, you know, so you kind of have to make the most of every moment you've got. If you go around avoiding everything to try and stay safe, you could end up not really living at all.'

The remains of their meal had been totally forgotten. The atmosphere between them was suddenly charged. As if challenges had been issued. Or an invitation?

Cooper signalled a waitress and paid for their meal. They walked outside and across the road but then paused. Fizz needed to go in one direction to her apartment. Cooper needed to head back towards the central city to flag down a taxi if he didn't want to walk all the way home. The vibrancy of restaurants and bars, with their bright lights and music, was behind them and the dark waters of the harbour were in front of them, with small boats bobbing on their moorings and a glimmer of moonlight on the ripples.

Neither of them moved.

Because neither of them wanted to say goodnight and walk away?

Cooper seemed fascinated by the harbour view, staring at it for a long moment. And then he turned to stare at Fizz and the eye contact sent a shiver down her spine.

'Thank you for sharing your story,' he said quietly. 'Am I wrong in thinking that it's not something you normally tell people you've just met?'

'I've never told anyone. Not about the adrenaline junkie stuff, anyway.'

He was shaking his head. 'I've never met anyone like you. And, yeah… I do think there's something wild about you but it feels good to be around you. As if that adrenaline high somehow rubs off a little bit.' He was smiling now. 'Maybe you're right. Maybe it would be good for me to try something like bungee jumping. Just once.'

Fizz let her breath out in a huff. 'But you're not going to, are you?'

'Probably not.'

'You're a wimp.'

'I'm safety conscious.'

'You're…' But any other teasing remark died on Fizz's lips as she still held his gaze. 'You're…' It was her turn to shake her head. 'I don't actually know,' she admitted, in a whisper. 'What *is* it about you, Cooper Sinclair?'

'I was asking myself the same thing about you. But I think I've figured it out now. It's the way you embrace life and get the most out of every moment.'

Fizz felt like she was falling into those eyes, which was crazy because she was still looking up. He was *so* tall. So solid and safe. She could feel herself leaning a little, even though she could swear she hadn't moved. Or maybe she had and that was why Cooper put his hands on her shoulders to steady her.

Her mouth felt suddenly dry.

'I don't do relationships, Coop.'

'I'm not looking for one,' he said. 'Especially not with someone I work with.'

'Good.' Fizz dipped her head in a single nod. 'That's that, then.'

'Yeah…'

But neither of them was breaking that eye contact. This had become another 'almost kiss' and this was what that sense of challenge had been about as they'd ended their meal, wasn't it?

A challenge to take a risk. Flirt with the danger of something that could go pear-shaped and make life difficult for both of them when they had to work together. But it was also about living for the moment and making the most of every one of them, and wasn't that what Cooper found attractive about her? And kissing this man held the promise of being a moment like none other in Fizz Wilson's life.

She could feel the heat of Cooper's hand on her shoulders seeping through her clothing and branding her skin. All she had to do to initiate this kiss would be to stand on tiptoe and tilt her face. All Cooper would have to do was to bend his head.

It seemed like they both decided to move at exactly the same time so their mouths met with a little more force than Fizz had been anticipating but that was as thrilling as the touch of Cooper's lips and, within a heartbeat, it wasn't enough. She lifted her hands to cradle his head and pull it even closer. To tempt his tongue to dance with hers. The force of desire that was being unleashed was like nothing Fizz had ever experienced and she felt like she was melting when Cooper's hands slid down her back to circle her buttocks and pull *her* closer.

The strength in those hands… Her feet came off the ground and it was the most natural thing in the world to wrap her legs around his waist, feeling one of her shoes falling off as she did so. She felt Cooper's arms come around her back to hold her safely and then he was turning in a circle, as if this was some kind of dance step. She could feel the huff of his surprise that became laughter beneath her lips but they didn't stop kissing.

The cheer that came from a group of young men heading into a nearby bar was a reminder that they were in a public place. Cooper loosened his hold. Fizz slid down to get her feet back on the ground.

'Oops… Sorry 'bout that.'

'I'm not.' There was still a hint of laughter in his tone.

Fizz ducked her head. She wasn't sorry, either, but she kept her gaze on ground level so she didn't reveal quite how *not* sorry she really was. 'Where's my shoe?'

'Right here, Cinderella.'

She stood on one foot as she slipped her shoe back on. 'I think it's time to go home.'

'That's probably very sensible.'

Fizz turned and took a step. And then another.

And then she turned back and held out her hand. She didn't say anything by way of invitation to come home with her but she didn't need to. Cooper returned her smile and reached out to take her hand. He was already moving in the same direction.

CHAPTER SIX

THEY WERE PRACTICALLY RUNNING, hand in hand, by the time they reached the harbourside apartment block where Fizz lived. By tacit agreement, they decided that waiting for the elevator to take them to the fifth floor was going to take too long, so they took the stairs— two at a time.

Both Cooper and Fizz were thoroughly out of breath by the time she slid her key into the lock and pushed her door open. Cooper pushed it shut behind him with his foot. He couldn't turn to use his hand because Fizz had turned and stopped, right in front of him—so close that her body was touching his and she was already reaching to drape her arms around his neck. Even as he heard the door click shut behind him, Cooper's lips were already on hers. He'd caught her hands and was now holding them above her head as he pressed her against the wall and kissed her as thoroughly as he'd ever kissed any woman in his life.

The heat of her mouth. The *taste* of her. The way she was arcing her body against his as if she wanted to feel every possible square inch of him that she could. Cooper let go of her hands a short time later, unable to resist the urge to touch more of her. When he reached the hem of her shirt and slipped his hands beneath to find the silky-soft skin of her belly, Fizz groaned into his mouth and pulled away. She wriggled against him, taking hold of her shirt hem herself and pulling it up, over her head, to drop it on the floor.

No, she didn't simply drop it. Fizz hurled it to one side and then turned her attention to the T-shirt Cooper was wearing beneath his leather jacket, grabbing the hem and hauling it up. Cooper's breath caught as he felt her hands brush his skin, his nipples hardening so fast it was painful enough for his breath to escape in a sound of astonishment.

Fizz paused instantly. She brought her face close to Cooper's, her lips and then her tongue brushing his before she spoke in a hoarse whisper.

'Too wild for you?'

'Are you kidding?' Cooper's breath came out in a groan this time. Then he scooped Fizz into his arms, one arm around her back, the other catching her behind the knees. 'Which way?' he demanded.

'Straight ahead.' Fizz was laughing. 'Last door on the left.'

The curtains were not drawn on the large window in her bedroom. City lights nearby and the sparkle of moonlight on the harbour in the background gave more than enough illumination for Cooper to aim safely for the centre of the large bed, where he dropped Fizz hard enough to make her bounce against the mattress.

She was still laughing as she unbuttoned her jeans and started wriggling out of them.

'You've got a wild streak yourself, Coop. That was a bit caveman, wasn't it?'

'Maybe you inspire me.' Cooper was shedding his

own clothes. He climbed onto the bed, looming over Fizz as she lay there wearing only her underwear now. Slowly he lowered his head so that he could kiss her again—this time as gently as he could. The flames of a passion that was barely controllable were licking all around them but he wanted to slow this down and make it last as long as he possibly could.

Fizz didn't do relationships. For all he knew, this could be a one-off and, if that was the case, Cooper intended to take a leaf out of her book and enjoy every single moment of it.

Dear Lord…

The very first impression that Fizz had ever had of Cooper was that he was a great big bear of a man. The sheer size of him should have been intimidating, especially given that his bulk was pure muscle. She had never been as aware of that muscle and the strength behind it as when he'd picked her up as if she weighed nothing to carry her to her bedroom. To get dropped like that, with enough of a gap beneath her to make her bounce on her mattress, should have been a warning that she was actually powerless against this man.

Totally vulnerable, in fact.

And yet…even when he was looming above her and she could feel the heat coming from his skin and the musky scent of arousal all around them, Fizz still felt safe. Well…as safe as anybody could feel when it was obvious she was about to jump off a precipice into a kind of sexual experience she just knew would be nothing like anything she had ever experienced before.

Maybe because she wasn't trying to control this.

How could she? In one instant, she was ready to explode with the power of her desire and wanted nothing more than for Cooper to speed this up and take them both over the edge but then, in the next instant, he was pulling back and touching and kissing her with a tenderness that broke her heart but was so compelling she never wanted it to stop.

It was a roller-coaster ride like no other.

A ride that had all the excitement of the kind of adrenaline rush that a brush with danger could deliver. But it was so much more than that. So much deeper.

It was like the thrill of danger while being wrapped up in the safest place imaginable. Within the circle of strong arms that could protect you from anything and gentle hands that could coax a thrill into pure ecstasy. It tapped into longings that Fizz would never admit to having, even to herself. And she didn't need to, because this kind of closeness, despite being only temporary, was enough to satisfy any unspoken longing.

Once wasn't enough for either of them so it was no real surprise when Fizz eventually caught a glimpse of her digital clock and found it was nearly three a.m.

'Oh, no...'

'What?' Cooper lifted his head from the pillow at her tone.

'I have to be on base at six a.m.'

'Me, too. Hey...maybe we'll get crewed together.'

Fizz wriggled out of the circle of Cooper's arms enough to be able to prop herself up on one elbow.

'People can't know,' she warned.

'They might notice,' Cooper said. 'If we're, like... on the same helicopter together.'

'I don't mean work. I mean what happens out of

work stays out of work, okay? I don't want anyone thinking I jumped on the new guy two minutes after he arrived. That's hardly professional. You never know, I might want to apply for one of the full-time HEMS positions one day.'

'I think the truth is more like we jumped on each other.' Cooper smiled. 'And it's been two weeks, not two minutes.'

'And that makes it okay?'

'I reckon.' Cooper was smiling again.

'What are you looking so pleased about?' Fizz frowned. 'I mean it, Coop. I don't want people talking about us. Speculating that this is anything more than what it is.'

'Which is?'

Fizz sighed. 'An inexplicable but apparently irresistible attraction between two adults who are entitled to do what they like as long as they're not hurting anyone else.'

'Ah… That sounds like an eloquent description.'

'Why are you still smiling?'

'Because…' Cooper reached out to brush a long lock of Fizz's hair back from her face and tuck it behind her bare shoulder. 'I thought it might be a one-off kind of thing for you and I'm happy that you're not using the past tense when you're talking about it. You said "happens" out of work, not "happened".'

'I don't do one-night stands,' Fizz told him. 'That's tacky.'

'But you don't do long term, either.'

'Define long term?'

'A relationship.'

'No, that's true.' Fizz lay back against her pillow

with another sigh. 'I don't do relationships. They imply a shared future. Making plans. I did that, once. I have the T-shirt. The one that says *"It doesn't matter what anybody promises you even when you trust them to keep those promises—the future's not a given, and it can disappear in the blink of an eye"*. And it can make your whole life feel like it's disappeared along with it. I'm not about to go through that again. Ever.'

'So…' Cooper sounded thoughtful. 'If this wasn't a one-night stand and it's not the start of a relationship, what is it?'

'Does it need a label? It is what it is. Living for the moment and enjoying something while it lasts. Moving on with no regrets when it stops being fun.' She rested her head against his shoulder. 'That's not a bad thing, is it?'

'Hell, no…sounds like every man's dream.'

'Because you don't do relationships, either?'

'I didn't say that, exactly. I said I wasn't looking for one.'

'But you've had them before? You're not like some international playboy type? Breaking hearts left, right and centre all over the world by delivering fabulous sex and then moving on?' Not that she believed a word of what she was suggesting. Cooper Sinclair was in no way a playboy type. He was too solid. Too sincere.

His laughter was a deep rumble in his chest that Fizz could feel as much as hear.

'Fabulous, huh?' His hand moved to slide across her body, brushing her breasts gently. Fizz should have been sated to the point of total exhaustion but the tendrils of sensation that his touch created told her that she was wrong. She might have had enough for one night but, overall, she hadn't had nearly enough of being with this man. 'And there I was, thinking that *you* were the fabulous one.'

'Hmm... Are you trying to avoid answering my question?'

'About relationships? No. I've moved around too much for anything to get serious. I'm nowhere near ready to settle down. Or maybe I've just got a short attention span. I'm always looking for a new adventure. A new challenge.'

A beat of something like anxiety caught Fizz. She had no idea how long it might take for the novelty of this new and astonishing type of physical adventure to wear off because she'd never experienced it before. How long would someone with a short attention span want it to continue before they were off looking for a new challenge?

'As long as they're safe, huh?' Fizz murmured. 'I wasn't a bit surprised that you carry condoms in your wallet, you know.'

'You wouldn't take risks with sex, would you?' He sounded worried.

'Of course not.' Fizz could feel her eyes starting to drift shut. 'I don't take stupid risks, you know. They're always well calculated.'

'Hmm...'

'You really got affected by that guy, didn't you?'

'What guy?'

'The one you worked with that you told me about. The partner who didn't follow the safety rules and got killed?'

'Ah...yeah, you could say that. He wasn't someone I worked with, though.'

Fizz was on the verge of falling asleep. 'Who was he, then?'

'My brother,' Cooper said, very quietly. 'My twin brother.'

The possibility of sleep vanished in an instant. Fizz felt her whole body tense, becoming alert as if a sudden danger had presented itself, but holding very still, as if it was trying to decide between fight or flight as a response to something shocking.

Fizz chose neither of those reactions. Instead, she turned her head to press her face against Cooper's chest. To feel his heartbeat beneath her cheek and the softness of his skin beneath her lips.

'I'm so sorry,' she whispered. 'I can only imagine how hard that must have been for you.'

'I think you know better than most people,' Cooper responded.

His arm pulled her a little closer and then they both lay there in silence. They should be trying to catch some sleep before they needed to go to work. Cooper needed to get home and be able to go to work in his own vehicle so that people wouldn't guess he'd hooked up with a work colleague so soon after arriving at a new job.

But this was a connection that Fizz didn't want to break.

For her own sake as much as for Cooper's.

No wonder it felt like he 'got' her more than other people did. He knew exactly what it was like to lose someone you were that close to. Someone you'd believed would be a huge part of the rest of your life.

This was a connection that was way more powerful than sharing a passion for their careers. Or the fact that sexually they were apparently a perfect match. This went so much deeper. Soul deep, in fact, because they both knew what it was like to have your world destroyed and have to pick it up again, piece by tiny piece. To come out of that process with the kind of scars that made it feel that it would be impossible to ever get that close to anybody else, ever again.

To have that in common made this even more perfect. Neither of them was looking for anything serious because they both had barriers that were too strong to let that happen. They could, however, enjoy each other's company. Enjoy working *and* playing together. Living for the moment and enjoying every single one of them.

She didn't break the silence between them by asking questions about what had happened to cause such a tragedy. If Cooper wanted to tell her, he would. Right now, he seemed content to simply hold her close. She could hear his breathing slowing and his muscles softening. Maybe he was already asleep. Her alarm was set so Fizz decided she could do that, too. Sink into a couple of hours of sheer bliss, sleeping in the warmth and safety of Cooper's arms.

Content in the conviction that this might have been the first time they had been together like this but it wasn't going to be the last. Not if she had any choice in the matter, anyway.

How did Fizz pull that off?

Cooper was onto his second cup of Shirley's excellent coffee before he'd began feeling like he was totally on top of his game but Fizz looked as if she'd enjoyed a solid eight hours' sleep instead of the two and half they'd finally managed. Her face positively glowed and her eyes sparkled.

It had been a mad dash in the early hours of this morning so that he could get home and shower and then take his own vehicle to the base, as if nothing untoward had happened last night. As if he hadn't experienced the most mind-blowing sex of his entire adult life. He could still feel the physical connection between himself and Fizz—a kind of hum in the air that got more powerful the closer their bodies were to each other's, like when he walked past where she was sitting to put his coffee mug into the dishwasher.

'Have you had enough to eat, love?' Shirley asked.

'More than enough, thanks, Shirley. And you make the best porridge I've ever tasted.'

'Oh, go on with you...' Shirley flapped her tea towel in his direction but her cheeks were pink with pleasure. 'I don't have a drop of Scottish blood in me but I do know to soak the oats overnight.'

Cooper walked back past Fizz, who was reading the newspaper at the table and not taking any more notice of him than she normally would. Nobody here could possibly have any idea what had happened between them last night and if Fizz wanted to keep it a secret, that was fine by him. It made it all the more exciting, in fact.

He paused this time, however. To look over her shoulder and read the headline on the front page of the paper. It wasn't that he was particularly interested in the news, he was simply enjoying that electric hum in the air between them and wanted to test that crescendo effect. And, yes, as soon as he got a whiff of the scent of Fizz's hair, it went off the Richter scale.

Even better, when he saw Fizz closing her eyes in a long blink and taking in a breath as if she was smelling a particularly pleasant perfume, he knew that she was just as aware of the hum as he was.

It was Maggie she turned to speak to, however.

'How's Harrison this morning?'

'He was still asleep when I left. Poor little guy, he was a bit miserable last night when they got back from the hospital. Laura's taken a couple of days off work until he can get his light cast on and goes back to school. It's a stress she really doesn't need, so I said I'd do dinner tonight for everyone.' Maggie glanced up at Cooper. 'Will you be home?'

'I can't think of any reason I wouldn't be.'

One of Maggie's eyebrows rose and Cooper's heart sank a little. Had she been aware of him creeping back into the shared house this morning? Laura might well have told her that he and Fizz had gone out to dinner together. But Maggie was smiling as she turned her gaze back to Fizz.

'You're welcome, too, of course. I'm thinking tacos. And Mexican beer.'

'Count me in.' Fizz reached for her pager as the warning signal of an incoming call sounded in the staffroom.

Cooper's pager sounded at the same moment and, for the first time this morning, they made direct eye contact with each other that lasted more than a split second.

With a beat of what had to be relief, he realised that the hum had been switched off as effectively as if someone had pulled a plug from a socket. The awareness of being so close, along with the memories of

that unbelievable physical connection they'd discovered, had been dismissed. This was work, and he was
lucky enough to be crewed with Fizz, who was one of
the best in this business. That tiny instant of eye contact before they both headed towards the helipad told
him that Fizz was in exactly the same frame of mind.
A totally professional space where anything personal
that could interfere with their performance was simply not allowed. Didn't exist, even.

The call was to a small coastal community isolated
enough for the first response emergency team to have
been the local fire service. The house was so close to
the beach that the damp sand was the obvious place
to land.

'Tide's well out but we'll need to keep an eye on
time,' Andy warned them.

One of the fire officers was waiting for Cooper and
Fizz as they scrambled through sand dunes and tus-
socks on the edge of the beach.

'Sorry to call you all the way out here,' he said.
'There may not be much you can do.'

'Oh?' Fizz frowned. 'What's going on?'

'It's tricky. Ken—who runs a grocery store in the
nearest town—made a delivery for them this morning
and he was the one who called for help.'

They were almost out of the dunes now, heading for
a small house that looked like a typical New Zealand
bach, or holiday house, with bleached wooden clad-
ding and a corrugated-iron roof.

'So what's the problem?' Cooper asked.

'It's a young couple living here. Tim and Sarah
Poulson. He's terminal. Pancreatic cancer. Apparently

he's got a legally drawn-up "Do Not Resuscitate" order but Ken decided it's not right and something needs to be done. The local doctor got called but both he and the district nurse are tied up with a woman having a baby at the moment. The doc said if Tim's as bad as Ken seems to think he is, then maybe some extra help *is* needed.'

Fizz could now see a van parked in front of a fire engine on an unsealed road behind the tiny house and a man who was pacing back and forth, flanked by another two fire officers. She caught Cooper's glance as they got closer.

This was not like any job she'd been to before. She couldn't just rush in, geared up to save a life, because that clearly wasn't going to be possible. Even prolonging the life of this patient might not be the right thing to do. Disconcertingly, Fizz felt a little unsure of how to tackle this job.

Cooper didn't seem the least bit unsure. He went straight to the pacing man and put a hand on his shoulder.

'Ken?'

'Yeah… Thank goodness you got here so fast. He can hardly breathe, man…and it's…pretty horrible.'

Cooper nodded. 'Thanks for letting us know. We've got this now, okay? You don't need to worry. We'll do whatever's needed to help.'

Ken rubbed his forehead with his hand. 'Thanks… I… I couldn't just leave them like that, you know?'

'I know.' Cooper patted his shoulder. 'It's okay. You did the right thing.'

'But there's nothing more you can do, Ken,' one of the fire officers put in. 'Time you went home now, eh?'

Ken turned to stare at the front door of the house.

'It's okay,' Cooper said again. 'We've got this.'

Did they? Fizz followed Cooper through a garden of seaside plants, decorated with driftwood sculptures, and onto a porch that had a veranda festooned with windchimes made of shells. Normally, she would lead a crew into any scene she'd been called to, but this time she stayed half a pace behind Cooper because he seemed so calm. Confident. In complete control.

He took off his backpack of gear and left it on the veranda before tapping lightly on the door. Fizz followed his example with her pack. A quick glance over her shoulder, as she did so, showed her the delivery van was leaving and that the fire officers were all staying near their truck. She and Cooper were being left to deal with this situation alone.

'Sarah?' Cooper's call was quiet as he stepped inside. 'Air Rescue here. I'm Cooper and I've got Fizz, who's a doctor, with me.'

'Oh, no…' A young woman, probably only in her early twenties, appeared at an internal door. Her long blonde hair was hanging loose and her pale face was streaked with tears. 'I told Ken not to call anybody. Please…we just need to be left alone…' She covered her face with her hands and started sobbing.

Without hesitation, Cooper stepped forward and took her into his arms.

'It's okay,' he said softly. 'We're here to help you. And Tim, if he needs it, of course, but *you* as well. Have you got someone here supporting you?'

She shook her head. 'We…we decided that we wanted it to be…to be just the two of us when it came to the end…' She tried, and failed, to stifle another sob.

'But Ken told me it wasn't right. That I had no right to just…to just let Tim suffer like this…'

Cooper kept his arm around Sarah's shoulders. 'Where is he?' he asked. 'We can check him for you. We can see if he's in any pain and do something to help that.'

'He's been on a morphine pump for weeks now. And fentanyl patches. He was awake a while ago and we watched the sun come up together and he said he wasn't in any pain but…he's not awake now and his breathing sounds awful…'

The main room of this small house had sliding doors that made the whole wall glass and it provided a view across the sand dunes and out to sea. The doors were open a little and the wash of the waves breaking created a gentle background song. A big bed had been positioned in the centre of the room where Sarah's husband, Tim, was propped up on pillows.

'These are his notes.' Sarah handed a file of papers to Fizz. 'The doctor visited yesterday and the district nurse helped me with all the medications. His DNR paper is in there, too. He really doesn't want to be… to be…'

'I understand.'

It was clear to Fizz that this patient was going to die very soon. His breathing did sound very distressed but a gentle examination after she'd quickly scanned all his notes told her that Tim was as comfortable as possible. It was the rattle of accumulating fluid that was making his breathing sound so upsetting for Sarah and she had medication that could help with that.

Cooper came close as she was drawing up the medication into a syringe. 'I'm going to call Andy and tell him we may be here for a while,' he said quietly. 'I don't want to intrude but I don't think we can leave Sarah without support.'

'Of course not.' It could be a matter of minutes but it could be hours. Cooper had to be aware of the kind of costs involved in keeping a rescue crew out of action but, if he was, he wasn't going to let it stop him doing what he felt was the right thing to do.

And he knew exactly how to handle this situation. He helped Sarah adjust Tim's pillows and to wipe his face and put salve on his lips.

'This is the most beautiful place,' he said quietly. 'So peaceful.'

'It was Tim's family's bach,' Sarah told him. 'When he knew he was going to die, this was where he wanted to be. Where he'd had so much fun on summer holidays when he was a kid. It was where we met... I was staying with friends up the beach a bit when I was fifteen. He was seventeen and...and...' She had tears rolling down her face. 'And I don't know what to do now... I thought I would but I don't because it's just too hard...'

'Okay...' Cooper's voice was calm. 'Come and sit on the bed, beside Tim. Lie down beside him if that feels right. Hold his hand. Or cuddle him. Talk to him. He can probably hear you but, even if he can't, he'll know you're here with him.'

'Really?' Sarah's whisper was another sob but Cooper nodded.

'I think so.' He took her hand and helped her climb onto the bed.

'The thing Tim needs right now is to be held by someone who loves him.' Cooper's voice was so gentle that Fizz felt the sting of tears in her eyes. 'It's what he needs and it's what you need, too, Sarah.'

Sarah had her head on the pillows beside Tim's and she was wrapping her arms around her husband.

'We're going to leave you alone,' Cooper added quietly. 'If that's what you want.'

'It's…it's what I promised but…but I'm scared…'

'I know.' Cooper touched her arm. 'But we'll be close. If you need anything at all, just call, okay? We'll hear you.'

The danger of her tears escaping had Fizz out of the room before Cooper. This wasn't her. She dealt with life-threatening emergencies and she had dealt with death on many occasions. And, yes, of course she felt sad when she lost a patient. Devastated, sometimes. But she didn't dissolve into tears. Ever. She'd decided years ago that she'd simply used up her lifetime supply of them when Hamish had been killed. Having to blink away the extra moisture in her eyes in this moment was…well…it was strange enough to be disturbing.

She wandered away from the road, where the fire truck had been joined by a police car now. Round the corner of the house, she could sit on a driftwood log that was just to one side of the glass doors of the main room. She could see the beach and the soothing curl of the breaking waves and would hear if she was called for some reason, but she could also stay out of view of where Tim and Sarah were sharing such an intense and tragic farewell.

That was why she was in bits, Fizz decided. It was all just too close to home. A young couple being forced apart for ever, with all their hopes and dreams for the future being torn away at the same time.

There was room on the log for Cooper when he came to find her a few minutes later.

'Andy's on a park a few miles up the coast. If he's needed for an emergency, he'll take off back to the city but come and get us later.'

Fizz nodded. 'I don't think we'll be here all that long.'

'No.'

There was a wealth of things being left unsaid in that short word. The acknowledgement that a young life was ending. That there was nothing they would be able to do to help with all the grief and disruption to lives that was happening and would continue for a very long time. But Cooper had already done so much to help. The depth of his understanding of exactly what to do in such an intense situation had blown Fizz away. She still felt curiously overwhelmed and just a little bit wobbly.

'How did you know,' she asked quietly, 'how to handle that so well?'

Cooper was silent for a long moment. Then he took a deep breath and let it out in a slow sigh.

'I told you my brother died. My twin brother, Connor.'

Fizz nodded. She kept her gaze on Cooper's face but he wasn't looking at her. He leaned down and picked up a shell from the ground in front of them.

'We were sixteen,' he told her. 'Away for the weekend for some hiking and a bit of climbing in the Cairngorms, which is a gorgeous mountain range in the eastern highlands of Scotland. Connor got a bit carried away and took a risk with a ridge. Long story short, he fell and was critically injured. Chest and abdo injuries but mostly it was his head. He was unconscious from the moment he fell. There were other people nearby and they called for help and the next thing I knew, a helicopter was there and paramedics were trying to save Connor's life.'

There was another moment of silence in which Fizz could actually feel the depth of emotion Cooper was dealing with here. She wanted to take hold of his hand but he was still playing with that shell. Instead, she leaned a bit closer, so that her shoulder was touching his.

'I was standing there, watching them,' Cooper continued quietly. 'And, even though I knew nothing about anything medical, I could see that it wasn't going well. I'd seen enough TV shows to know what a flat line on a monitor screen meant, even if it wasn't there all the time. I could feel my world just falling away and I was going with it, into the most terrifying black hole that ever was.

'And…and then one of those paramedics came and put his arm around me and he explained what was happening and how hard they were trying to help Connor, and…it was a lifeline. Something I could hang onto so that I didn't disappear completely into that black hole. They were amazing, those guys. They got Connor to hospital alive and took me in the helicopter with them and made it seem like I was doing a really important job as well, just being with my brother and talking to him. Touching him. They told me he could probably hear me. That he would know I was there…'

Cooper dropped the shell and rubbed his face with his hand. 'That was when I decided I was going to become a paramedic,' he said. 'I thought, if I could ever offer that kind of lifeline to anyone in such an awful situation, it would be a really worthwhile thing to do.'

Fizz nodded. 'You did exactly that for Sarah,' she told him. 'You were…amazing…'

She caught Cooper's gaze as she spoke and suddenly she was completely caught. She couldn't look away. Because she could see so much of what he was feeling in his eyes? The kind of grief he understood so well. How much he cared for others. The sheer enormity of how kind this man was…

It was Cooper who broke the eye contact. 'I might just go and have a peep around the door,' he said, getting to his feet. 'Sarah won't know I'm there but I'd like to know that she's coping. It's romantic that they wanted to be alone together for this but…well…we both know how hard it can be, don't we?'

Fizz stayed where she was. Without thinking, she reached down and picked up the shell that Cooper had been toying with when he'd been telling her about his brother. She curled her fingers around its sharp edges.

It wasn't just Cooper's physical size that made him seem so solid, it was his personality. That kindness and caring made him completely trustworthy.

A human rock.

Weirdly, Fizz felt the sting of gathering tears for the second time that day. The second time that decade, probably.

This time it wasn't because of memories of grief. Maybe it was because of that feeling of longing a human rock could provoke—the desire to cling? Fizz had learned a long time ago not to cling to anything or anyone but how comforting would it be to have someone you *could* cling to if you needed to?

Whoever captured Cooper Sinclair's heart in the future would have a human rock for the rest of her life. Fizz could only hope that she would know how incredibly lucky she was.

Having lost of track of how long she'd been sitting on the log, the quiet call from Cooper startled her.

'Fizz?'

'Yes?' She still had the shell in her hand as she got to her feet. Without thinking, she slipped it into her pocket.

'He's gone. Sarah says it was very peaceful in the end. The police can take over and they're going to give her as much time as she needs before they make any arrangements to transport Tim, but we need you to do the official paperwork.'

'Of course.'

'The firies are going to take us to where Andy's got the chopper parked after that.' Cooper offered a lopsided smile. 'Have you had a ride in a fire engine before?'

'Can't say I have.' The next few minutes were not going to be easy. Having a moment of relief being offered was welcome. 'Working with you is just one big adventure, isn't it, Coop?'

'We've just got started, babe,' he murmured as they headed back to the door of the beach house. 'The best is yet to come.'

CHAPTER SEVEN

COOPER WASN'T THE only one who could provide a bit of adventure.

Not that Fizz had initially had that intention when she'd offered to take him sightseeing when one of their days off coincided a couple of weeks later.

'I thought you might like to visit Featherston, which isn't too far away and is a great example of a small New Zealand town. I happen to know where there's a really good place to have lunch.'

She knew every street of the town, in fact.

'This is where I grew up,' she told Cooper as they drove around after an excellent pub lunch of fish and chips. 'In that house right there.' She stopped the car as they both gazed at the small weatherboard cottage. It was disappointing to see that the garden was so overgrown. 'My grandfather built it. My mother was born there.'

'And she inherited the house? Is that why you grew up there?'

'No.' Fizz pulled away again, heading for the town's main street. 'My grandparents brought me up. Well, my nan did, mostly. Grandpa died when I was about ten.'

Cooper's glance was sharp. Cautious. Was he worried that he might say or do something inappropriate? Did he expect to feel mortified very soon—the way he had when he'd misunderstood why her marriage had been so short-lived?

'My mother's not dead,' Fizz reassured him. 'I'm just not actually that close to her. She got pregnant far too young and decided she still wanted to have a life. She'd pop home occasionally and promise that she'd come and get me as soon as she'd got herself settled somewhere but it never quite happened. As far as I know, she's living happily with her third husband somewhere in Australia. I was the one who inherited the house but I sold it to pay my way through medical school.'

She glanced sideways at some of the newly refurbished buildings they were passing on the main street. 'I should have kept it. Property prices have had a very healthy increase since people realised that it was in easy commuting distance of Wellington but... I guess it felt like there wasn't much keeping me here. Especially after Nan died.'

She didn't let a silence develop to where Cooper might start feeling sorry for her. Or to start feeling sorry for herself, for that matter. It wasn't pleasant to remember those crushing childhood disappointments. Those promises her mother had always made but never kept. Visits that she was going to make. Holidays that they were going to take together. A new home to go to with a new husband so that they could all live together happily ever after.

'Hey...' Fizz stamped on the ancient echoes of being

let down. 'How 'bout we do something a bit more exciting before we go home?'

Cooper gave her a slightly wary look. 'I know what "exciting" means in your vocabulary. Does this involve the need for protective clothing of any sort?'

'No.' Fizz threw him a grin. 'You don't even need to get out of the car if you don't want to.'

'Where are we going?'

'Somewhere cool. With a bit of a breeze probably, which will blow a few cobwebs away.' Like the ones that seemed to be hiding in the corners of her old home town. And her heart. 'You up for it?'

His glance was thoughtful now. As if he was weighing up what she'd said. 'Why not?' He finally nodded. 'It's always good to blow cobwebs away.'

There was indeed a stiff sea breeze when they arrived at Ocean Beach after a picturesque drive mainly though farmland. She showed him the quaint, weathered little holiday houses that stretched along part of the beach and then took him on a track she'd been on before with the four-wheel-drive club. The road got rough enough at times to make Fizz focus hard on her driving, especially when there was a steep drop on the beach side as they wound their way around the edge of a hill. There was a deeply rutted track through trees with puddles big enough to send up a wall of muddy water and rocky streams to navigate, which bounced them around and made them both laugh with the fun of it all.

Finally, Fizz parked on the rock-strewn black sand, amongst all the driftwood, and got out of the car to breathe in the salty air and watch the wild waves crashing onto this deserted shore.

Cooper got out as well.

'Where are we exactly?'

'That's Palliser Bay out there.' Fizz pointed out to sea. 'And the South Island is that way, only it's a bit too far to see from this point.'

Cooper turned his head, taking in the endless beach, the rugged green hills of the farmland nearby and the distant peaks of the Rimutakas in the background.

'It's gorgeous,' he said. 'Reminds me of Scotland.'

'Are you homesick?'

'Not at all. There's nothing there for me now.'

He turned back towards the sea but Fizz was still looking at him. She was curious, she realised. She wanted to know what he'd meant by that or, rather, how he felt about that. She had been shocked to learn about his twin brother's death and how terrible it must have been for Cooper. On top of the case they were attending to at the time, it had been such an emotional day Fizz had needed a bit of time to process it all. Even now, she could feel a lump forming in her throat. She stepped over a pile of sun-bleached branches and went to sit on the trunk of an entire driftwood tree with its roots still intact.

Cooper came to sit beside her a couple of minutes later. 'You okay?' he asked. 'You've gone kind of quiet.'

Fizz caught his gaze and, instantly, she was reminded of how she'd seen him that first day. As a human rock. Trustworthy. As trustworthy as Hamish had been and he'd been the first person, apart from her grandparents, that she could trust to keep his word.

'I was just thinking about the last time we were near

a beach together,' she said quietly. 'I've been wondering quite a lot about how Sarah's coping.'

'Hopefully she's got family and friends who are helping her.'

'Mmm.'

'Did you?' Cooper slung his arm around her shoulders in a companionable gesture. 'Have plenty of support when you needed it? When Hamish died?'

It felt so natural to tilt her head to find the comfortable hollow beneath his shoulder. 'I think I pushed people away,' she admitted. 'They were all there for the funeral, of course. Even my mother. And Hamish's parents were great and… I know they didn't blame me for the accident but it felt like I reminded them of what they'd lost every time they saw me. That they'd never see their son become a father. Or see their grandchildren grow up. They just kind of faded out of my life, I guess. And my friends stopped trying after a while.'

She'd told him about what had made her become an adrenaline junkie but she'd skated over that dark period. It was another thing she'd never told anybody.

'Sometimes,' she added quietly, 'what you're feeling is so powerful it sucks you in and it makes you push away anything that tries to pull you out. If you push often enough and hard enough, most people will go away eventually.'

'Not the people who really love you,' Cooper said. 'You might think you've pushed them away but they're always ready to come back.'

'You sound like you're speaking from personal experience.'

'Perhaps. I didn't push people away. I think I was

the one who got pushed. Until I felt I had to hide so I didn't make everything worse.'

Fizz tilted her head to look up at Cooper's face. 'I don't understand.'

'You know how you told me that when Hamish died, it felt like someone had taken your life and screwed it up and thrown it away?'

She nodded.

'It was the same for me. Only it was even worse for my mother. She never got over losing Connor.'

'They didn't *blame* you, did they?'

'No more than I blamed myself. We all knew that Connor was headstrong, and sometimes he just wouldn't listen, but the "if onlys" were hard to get past. If only we hadn't gone climbing that weekend. If only it hadn't been raining earlier. If only I'd paid more attention to what he was doing instead of trying to light a fire to cook the breakfast sausages over. If only we hadn't looked so much like each other...' Cooper blew out a breath. 'Every time my mother looked at me, I knew she was seeing Connor. Sometimes she'd actually go pale and then collapse with grief all over again.'

Fizz had found Cooper's hand and she threaded her fingers through his. Had Cooper never been able to express his grief at losing his brother because he'd been trying to protect his mother? She could believe that about him. He would protect anybody he loved to the nth degree. But how sad was it to have felt the need to hide his own emotions like that?

'It got so that it was easier to avoid being at home,' Cooper added. 'It was such a relief to get away to university and then to have my career to focus on.'

Had he become even better at hiding his emotions

by focusing so completely on his study and career? Fizz knew how well that worked. She barely thought about any of those heart-breaking regrets these days— like never being able to create the kind of family she'd desperately wanted as a child. A 'real' family.

'Your parents must have been very proud of you, taking up a career that was going to save lives.'

'My dad died just before I graduated. And Mum seemed to fade away over the next few years. Every time I went to visit, she was thinner and sadder and there didn't seem to be anything I could do or say that would help. Her doctors couldn't find any way to help her, either. I think she just gave up on life.'

Fizz squeezed his hand but didn't say anything for a long moment. Curiously, it felt like something was shifting in her chest. A piece of her heart? As if a door was being opened somewhere when she had believed that the key had been lost long ago, because the connection to this person was so strong she couldn't keep Cooper out.

This friendship was special.

It felt…

Well, it felt a bit like family. One of those 'real' ones.

There was a lot to be said for the philosophy of living in the moment, making the most of every one of them and not trying to think too far into the future.

That day off a week or two ago, when Fizz had taken Cooper to see the small town where she'd grown up and then taken him on that wild drive to that beautiful beach, was a shining example of that philosophy.

They'd made the most of that day. Looking back, it

had been an extraordinarily intimate conversation, unlike any Cooper had ever had. Was that because he'd never had a friend like Fizz? Someone that could understand how profound the effect of losing someone so close could be? He'd had no idea how much of a release it could be, just telling someone about something, either. He'd never spoken to anyone about how hard it had been after Connor had died but, then, he'd never had someone like Fizz to talk to, had he?

It had certainly brought them closer and Cooper was making the most of every moment he had with Fizz, along with all the other good things his new life was offering him. Within the space of just a few short months his old life in Scotland was feeling like a lifetime ago.

He knew his way around this quirky, hilly city well enough to be able to speed to any emergency he was dispatched to if he was crewing one of the vehicles, and he'd discovered how lucky he'd been to find a place to live in such an interesting part of town. The atmosphere of the rambling old house he was sharing with Maggie, Jack, Laura and Harrison was relaxed enough for no comment to be made when he was out very late, or quite often didn't come home at all.

The Mexican night with tacos and beer had been such a success that it had become a weekly thing, with each flatmate taking turns to provide the meal for whoever wasn't on a night shift. Cooper found opportunities to kick a ball around the back yard with Harrison, whose broken wrist was completely healed now, and there were always occasions to share the kitchen or some housework, along with work stories, with Jack or Laura. Maggie was rostered on the same shift at the rescue base often enough for a real friendship to be developing but, if she'd guessed that Cooper had something going on with Fizz, she wasn't saying anything.

That 'something' that had started as a fierce and irresistible sexual attraction was quite a different 'something' now. It had changed the day of that case when they'd stayed to support Sarah as her husband had died in her arms. And it had changed again that day on the beach when they'd shared how hard life had been after losing the people closest to them. There seemed to be a level of trust now, on both sides, that might have otherwise taken a much longer time to develop.

In its turn, that level of trust had taken their sexual connection to a new level. Cooper didn't have to remind himself to make the most of every moment when it came to the intimate time he and Fizz managed to find at least once or twice a week when their rosters co-operated. It was, without a shadow of doubt, the best sex he'd ever had in his life and he suspected that that had a lot to do with Fizz's philosophy on life.

There was no pressure to put a label on what they had found with each other and there were no expectations that whatever it was was 'going somewhere', which had got in way of a lot of previous relationships for Cooper. He'd been dumped in the past because a relationship was apparently 'not going anywhere', or he'd had to walk away from someone himself because of the building pressure to take a relationship seriously enough, but that wasn't going to happen with Fizz. He was with someone who was in exactly the same place he'd always been as far as relationships were concerned, even if he'd never really analysed that reluctance to commit.

Maybe he could see his attitude to commitment changing at some point in the future but he certainly wasn't ready to settle down yet and take responsibility for someone else's happiness. He was even less ready to consider having a family and taking responsibility for the health and safety of vulnerable children.

He'd told Fizz that his parents hadn't blamed him for his brother's death any more than he blamed himself and that was true but it didn't mean that there wasn't an element of blame to be found. He'd been the older brother. Only by thirty minutes, admittedly, but he'd been expected to be the responsible one. To take care of Connor and make sure he didn't do anything stupid.

He hadn't managed that very well, had he?

Even now he would have that terrible recurring dream sometimes. When he was shouting at Connor to tell him to come down off the rocks because they were too slippery and it was too dangerous but no sound could emerge, no matter how much effort he was making to force the words out. Even worse was reliving that moment when he got close enough to touch his brother's crumpled body at the base of those rocks and to feel the fear and grief exploding within his chest as if it had just happened all over again.

Whoa... Cooper shook that thought off with practised ease, taking note of what had prompted it so he could try and avoid it in the future. Thinking about having a family and children of his own, that's what it had been. He'd told Fizz that he wasn't looking for a relationship because he wasn't ready to settle down. Given how his brain had just hijacked him with no more than a passing thought of having children of his own, Cooper had to wonder whether he would ever be ready to settle down like that.

He'd also told Fizz that enjoying something like this while it lasted and then moving on with no regrets when it stopped being fun was every man's dream and he'd meant every word of that as well. And now he was living that dream and it *was* perfect.

The fact that he was on the same page as Fizz at the moment, as far as settling down or having kids went, was a good thing.

It meant that they could just carry on. Enjoying every moment.

Work was pretty close to perfect, too. Cooper wasn't sure if Fizz had said something to Don or that someone else had noticed how well they worked together as a team but he was finding himself crewed with Fizz on one of the helicopters every time she was on base, and that was another aspect of his life that he was making the most of. The challenge of keeping up with how fast this young doctor thought and worked was a joy and there were always new things to learn. Fizz was learning from him as well. He was helping her prepare for her upcoming winch training course and, because she'd also signed up for the high country and mountain rescue course in Queenstown, he was sharing some of his knowledge in that area as well.

'We've only got a couple of weeks before we head to Queenstown,' he reminded her as they were airborne on the way to an incident that was a thirty-minute flight away from Wellington. A slightly hysterical call to emergency services had said a large vehicle—maybe a truck or a bus—had gone off the road and into a gully but the crew were still waiting for information on how bad it was and how many people were involved. They had been dispatched because the location was isolated and there was the potential for serious injuries and an unknown number of victims, but it could turn out to be less than serious or even a hoax. 'Did you read that article I sent you the other day?'

'The one about hazards? Yeah... I had a quick look.'

'So, what are they?'

'The hazards?' Fizz raised an eyebrow. 'Weather, mainly. Storms, lightning, risk of hypothermia. Oh, and there's avalanches and rockfalls, of course. And river crossings and white water. Hey...do we get to do an actual river crossing on this course, do you think? Where you can tackle a swift current by linking arms?'

'I think we might. We're expected to take quite a lot of outdoor clothing.'

'Layers.' Fizz nodded. 'I read that bit, too. Lightweight clothes that can wick moisture away from the body, insulating items for the middle like a top made of merino wool and then a waterproof layer on top. I might go to one of those tramping supplies shops after work today and get some new thermal stuff. Want to come with me?'

'Sure.'

'We could go somewhere for dinner afterwards.'

Fizz wiggled her eyebrows this time, as she held his gaze, and Cooper had to stifle laughter. It was just as well Andy couldn't see into the cabin of this helicopter or he'd know instantly that he and Fizz were a lot closer than simply friends or colleagues. The longer it took for anybody to guess, the better, as far as Cooper was concerned. It was nobody's business but theirs and it didn't interfere with how they worked together. If anything, it just seemed to be making them a tighter team.

Yep. Things were pretty much perfect on so many levels.

CHAPTER EIGHT

COOPER AND FIZZ could hear Andy talking on a different frequency as he flew them towards this new emergency of a large vehicle accident and then his voice came through the headphones built into their helmets.

'Okay, guys… First police and fire vehicles are on scene. It's a school bus that's crashed.'

Cooper and Fizz exchanged a brief glance. This was serious. It could be the worst job they might ever face. It wasn't a long glance but it was enough for a silent message of support and strength to be transmitted and received in both directions. They were in this together. They could cope.

'Nobody knows how many kids are on the bus,' Andy continued, 'but it was heading to school so it could be full. It's down a steep gully. Broke a few trees on the way down, which probably lessened the impact, but it's on its side and access is difficult. They're trying to get ladders down and make sure the bus is stable.'

Cooper saw a reflection in Fizz's face of his own increase in adrenaline levels and focus. This could be a Mass Casualty Incident that would be a real challenge to handle, especially when the victims might be young children.

'Comms said they've called for more backup for scene control. As you're qualified in disaster management, Cooper, they're putting you in as scene commander. You know where the vest is?'

'Roger that.' Cooper was already leaning towards the window, waiting for his first sighting of the scene. Getting an aerial view would be an advantage in deciding how to manage this disaster. As they circled the scene, coming down to land on the road a few minutes later, Cooper could already see how chaotic it was.

There were cars backed up in both directions and people running to where the bus had gone off the road on a bend, crowding the firies, who were trying to do their job. An ambulance was having trouble getting past the cars and closer to the scene, thanks to a tractor that was blocking it.

On foot, and moving swiftly towards a police officer who was trying to move people back from the edge of the road, Cooper realised that this crowd was mostly made up of the parents of the children in that bus. Women were crying. There were toddlers and babies in the crowd and the farmer who'd arrived on his tractor was arguing with the policeman.

'It's my kids down there. You can't tell me I can't go down and help.'

People turned to stare at Cooper and Fizz as they arrived. They could all read the lettering on his fluorescent vest that designated him 'Scene Commander'. Cooper knew his physical size helped give him authority in situations like this but he also knew it was more about confidence and giving frightened people the reassurance that he knew what he was doing.

The ambulance and its crew had finally got close

enough to park and open its back doors. Cooper quickly spoke to the chief fire officer, surveyed the scene and then gathered the paramedics and police officers.

'They're going to get access to the bus any minute now and they'll start bringing the children up. From what they can see so far, they don't think there's major injuries. The kids were all wearing their safety belts. We'll use the space beside the ambulance as the triage area. Dr Wilson will assess any serious injuries and we'll get another chopper on the way if it's needed. Given their age, everybody will need another check at the nearest hospital but we may be able to use road vehicles for transport, including the parents' cars.'

He turned to speak to the group of frantic adults and urged them to step back and give all the emergency service personnel room to work. Police officers reinforced his message and people were listening now. Some went to shift their cars and make sure there was room for more emergency vehicles to get through.

Cooper turned back to brief the paramedics on what their roles would be, but when he saw Fizz at the top of one of the fire service ladders he shook his head and strode towards her.

'No,' he said. 'Not this time, Fizz. Stay up here.'

'But…'

'No "buts".' He shifted his gaze to the fire officer beside them. 'There's no one unconscious in the bus, is there?'

'Not that we can see.'

'What about the driver?'

'She's been keeping them calm. She's trapped by her lower legs under the dashboard but she adamant that all the kids are taken out first. And she's told them all to stay still and keep their safety belts on until someone comes to get them, which is just as well what with the broken windows and sharp metal around. The smashed tree branches are another big hazard, like I was just telling the doctor, here.'

'She could be bleeding badly,' Fizz said. 'So could one of the children. I need to get down there…'

The fire officer was peering down the slope. 'First one's on its way up.'

'I need you here,' Cooper told Fizz, 'to assess each one of these children as they get brought up.'

He could see her frustration. She was determined to get down that slope. Her adrenaline levels were high and what Fizz wanted to do was to get into that wrecked bus as fast as possible.

Cooper kept his voice calm. 'You outrank me in medical matters,' he told her, 'but I'm the scene commander here and it's my responsibility to manage this scene as safely as possible. We've got people who know what they're doing, handling the extrications.'

'You're telling me I'm not allowed to go down there?'

Cooper nodded. 'Not unless there's a good medical reason for it. And, even if there is, I'm going to be the one who takes that risk, okay?'

He saw the flash of rebellion in her eyes but, as he held her gaze, Cooper also saw the moment that she accepted his authority and that felt like an even bigger step towards total trust. Tightening the bonds that were there between them as a professional team. Fizz's focus shifted as soon as a fire officer appeared at the top of the ladder, a small, sobbing child held against his chest. It was Fizz who reached to take the young girl, who barely looked old enough to have been heading to school.

'Come with me, sweetheart,' she said. The child wrapped her arms around Fizz's neck and buried her face against her shoulder. 'It's okay...' Cooper heard Fizz say gently as she moved towards the ambulance and the blankets that had been laid on the road as a triage area. 'You're safe now...'

'Jenny...?' A woman with a baby in her arms broke away from the group that was now gathered at more of a distance and ran towards Fizz. 'Oh, my God... Are you hurt?'

It took over an hour to get more than twenty young children safely out of the bus and up to road level, where Fizz was checking each one as thoroughly as she could. A dislocated elbow and a greenstick arm fracture seemed to be the most serious injuries amongst many bumps and bruises and a few grazes and lacerations, but, once each one was bandaged or splinted and comforted, they were taken to the nearest hospital for observation and another check-up. Cooper used a second ambulance that arrived to take the eight-year-old with the elbow injury and his mother to hospital and the well-splinted arm fracture got transported in a police car, much to the small boy's excitement.

The first girl who'd been rescued, Jenny, was still on scene as the final victim of the accident was brought up the side of the gully. Cheryl, the bus driver, was Jenny's grandmother and she was far more worried about the children she'd been driving than the badly broken ankle that had kept her trapped.

'They're all okay, Mum,' her daughter reassured Cheryl. 'And that's thanks to you making sure they always wore their safety belts.'

Fizz looked up from the IV line she had put in Cheryl's arm. 'How's the pain now?' she asked. 'On that scale of zero to ten?'

'About a four, I guess. A lot better, anyway.' But Cheryl was twisting her head sideways. 'Jenny? Are you sure you're okay, darling? Nothing hurts?'

'I got a big scratch, Nana, that's all. It's better now.'

'I can't believe it happened. There was something wrong with the brakes. I was trying to slow the bus using the gears but the wheel caught the gravel. *Oh...*' The sound was a sob. 'I could have *killed* someone.'

'But you didn't, Mum.' Her daughter was trying to lean close to comfort her mother but the crying baby in her arms was making it impossible.

'Here...let me help...' Fizz took the baby. She cuddled the six-month-old infant against her shoulder and patted its back. 'Hey...what's all this fuss about, huh?'

Jenny reached up to pat the baby as well. 'He's my little brother,' she told Fizz. 'His name's Patrick.'

Cooper had been splinting Cheryl's ankle as Fizz had managed the pain relief. Now Andy was helping him to secure their patient on the stretcher, ready to move her to the helicopter. He found himself glancing in Fizz's direction more than once. The baby had settled in her arms and Jenny was leaning against her legs. Andy was also looking at Fizz as he straightened up after fastening the last safety belt.

'Suits you.' He grinned.

Fizz grinned back. 'I don't think I've ever dealt with so many children in one go. I'm exhausted.'

Baby Patrick's mother smiled as she took her baby back. 'Thank you so much. You were wonderful with all the kids. Where will you take Mum?'

'To the Royal, in Wellington,' Cooper told her. 'We can fit you all in if you want to come with her.'

'No…don't do that, love,' Cheryl said. 'Patrick sounds like he's hungry. And you need to keep an eye on Jenny. I'll be fine…'

'Jenny should get another check-up at your local hospital,' Cooper told her. 'Like we've advised for all the other children.'

'I'll get in as soon as I can, then, Mum. I know you'll be well looked after with these guys.'

Finally back at base, after handing Cheryl over to the staff at the Royal's emergency department, Fizz flopped onto one of the sofas in the staffroom.

Andy sat at the table to open a packet of sandwiches and Cooper went to make coffee.

'We've got a heap of paperwork to get sorted,' he sighed. 'A patient report form on every one of those kids.'

'I'll ring the hospitals they got taken to, later,' Fizz said. 'I'd like to make sure I didn't miss anything. That was full on, trying to check so many small people.'

'You did great,' Andy told her. 'You're a natural with kids, Fizz. You'll make a great mum one of these days.'

'No, I won't.' Fizz made it sound like no big deal. 'I'm never going to have kids.'

Cooper spooned coffee into mugs. He couldn't agree more with Andy but he also remembered Fizz's response to Maggie's comment that day that her biological clock would start ticking before too long. He could still hear an echo of that dismissive laughter and the declaration that she would simply ignore any ticking of that clock because life was too much fun as it was.

But he'd seen her with that baby in her arms today and he'd seen the way she'd cuddled him and pressed a kiss to his head. Was her determination not to have children herself part and parcel of the same barrier that meant she didn't 'do' relationships?

How sad was that?

And not just for Fizz, Cooper realised as he stirred those mugs of coffee for longer than was necessary. He was aware of a wash of sadness that was far more personal.

Living for the moment was all very well but maybe it wasn't as perfect as he'd thought such a short time ago. It gave whatever their unlabelled connection was a shelf life, didn't it? It couldn't keep going the way it was because it would just morph into a relationship, especially when other people found out about what was going on between them. The question, even if unspoken, of whether or not it was serious or had a future would be hanging over them and Cooper could be quite sure that that would be the point where it stopped being fun for Fizz. When she would move on with no regrets and he would be expected to do the same.

Except that Cooper didn't want to move on. Maybe he wasn't ready to settle down and raise a family but he was nowhere near ready to call it quits on the time he got to spend with Fizz.

He carried a mug of coffee over to her and she thanked him with a smile and a glance that held his for a heartbeat. Like that silent communication in the helicopter earlier, it was so easy to read and respond to the message.

We did well today, didn't we?

We sure did.

We're just the best team, ever...

Absolutely...

But Cooper couldn't return that smile. That unexpected flash of sadness he'd just had had become something that felt more like...fear?

Maybe it had only been a matter of weeks but he couldn't imagine his life without this woman as a central part of it. He knew it was probably a forlorn hope but he didn't want Fizz to move on.

Ever...

His heart felt like it was squeezing itself into a knot and Cooper had to turn away before that ability to communicate with no words gave Fizz any idea what was going through his head right now.

Not just through his head. The realisation was in his blood. Getting sent to every cell in his body.

He loved her.

He was *in* love with Fizz.

He had, without doubt, found the person he wanted to spend the rest of his life with.

And the moment she knew that, their time together away from work would be over. There would be no more shared meals or moonlit walks around the waterfront. No more of those delicious hours in her bed and the reminder of how mutual that pleasure was in those private glances the next time they were together. Even working together would be different because that trust she had in him would be broken.

Cooper took his own mug of coffee towards the table, sitting down opposite Andy. He reached for the day's newspaper that he hadn't had a chance to look at yet, but the words were no more than a blur as his brain scrambled to find a solution to what was suddenly a very pressing problem.

Then his vision cleared. The answer was quite simple, really.

He just couldn't let Fizz find out how he felt. He was good at hiding strong emotions. Losing Connor had taught him that because his mother had been unable to cope with her own emotions so he hadn't been about to make it all so much worse by talking about or revealing his own. As he'd said to Fizz, he'd been pushed away and he'd had many years to hone the skill of hiding. And, yes, part of him knew that he might be making things worse in the long run by staying as close to Fizz as possible for as long as possible, but what choice did he have?

He couldn't walk away. Not voluntarily, that was for sure. And…maybe, if they could keep this going long enough, Fizz would get used to it. Change her mind, even? She was starting to really trust him, wasn't she? Maybe she would come to realise that they were perfect life partners. It wasn't as if he had a desire for his own kids any more than she did. Or even marriage, for that matter.

Cooper just wanted Fizz in his life. And in his bed.

Preferably for ever…

There was something different about Cooper today but Fizz couldn't quite put her finger on what it was.

He seemed a bit quieter as they walked around an exclusive outdoor clothing outlet that evening.

'How 'bout this? A merino blend camisole.' For thermal underwear it was quite pretty and lacy. 'Too girly?'

'Buy it.' Cooper nodded. His grin was pure cheekiness. 'That way, when we're crossing rivers or building shelters in the forest, I can imagine what you've got on under all those other layers. It'll keep me warm with no need for my jacket.'

Oh… That glint in his eyes was enough to make Fizz feel overly warm herself. Suddenly, she wanted to get this shopping expedition over with. To get home and get Cooper into her bed.

But there was still something nagging at the back of her mind when they headed to the checkout counter a little while later. A young couple was in the queue ahead of them and the guy had a baby in his arms about the same age as the baby Fizz had cuddled this morning. The baby was peeping over his father's shoulder and seemed fascinated by Cooper. It wasn't until the baby giggled that Fizz glanced sideways and caught the faces Cooper had been making to amuse the infant.

Had that huge job today with the school bus affected him more than she'd realised? Thinking back, Fizz remembered an odd moment, when they'd got back to base and he'd made her a coffee. For just a second, she'd had the impression that he was quite sad about something. Had working with so many children triggered memories of time with his brother, perhaps? Memories could often catch you unawares, sometimes at very inappropriate times. Not that it had happened for Fizz recently, mind you, but she could sympathise.

She also remembered the way he'd been with Harrison when Laura's young son had broken his wrist.

The thought that this big, gentle man would make the most amazing father was followed by another realisation that almost took Fizz's breath away.

That's what Cooper was really searching for, wasn't it?

He might think he'd come to the other side of the world simply for more adventure and career challenges but he didn't actually realise what it was he was looking for, did he? He just knew that there was something missing from his life.

He'd said that there was nothing left for him in Scotland now because his family was all gone. But he needed a family of his own, didn't he? A wife who would adore him as the rock in her life. Children that he could protect and keep safe to his heart's content.

Except that he blamed himself, at some level, for his brother's death, didn't he? There was a barrier there that he probably wasn't even aware of because the men she'd known hadn't usually tried to analyse that kind of thing, so she couldn't help but wonder if the same could be said of Cooper.

Fizz couldn't share that desire. For her, children were the ultimate planning for the future. Even before they were born, they brought with them so many hopes and dreams for the years to come. The promise of family and for ever. The promise that Hamish had given her and that she'd believed. But it had been a promise that had died along with the man who'd made it. You could only keep yourself safe from heartbreak if you didn't buy into hopes and dreams like that.

But perhaps she could help Cooper.

And why wouldn't she? He was just the loveliest man she had ever met and, hopefully, when their time together had run its course, she would still have a friend for life—one that she already cared about a great deal. Cooper was not just gorgeous, he was clever and kind and…pretty close to perfect, really. He deserved to have everything good that life had to offer, especially after having lived through the worst that it could also offer.

He'd said he'd never had a serious relationship because he'd moved around so much but Fizz suspected that it was because he didn't want to get that close to someone when he knew what it was like to lose them. She got it. More than anyone else could, probably. Fizz was content with her own decision to not have a family in her future but she understood now—in this moment of insight—that there was a real need, deep down, for Cooper to love and be loved. Somehow, he needed to break through the barrier that was holding him back. To find the courage to take that leap of faith in the future.

But how could she help him?

She put her purchases down to have them scanned and picked up the shop's catalogue. There was a montage of pictures on the cover that must have been shot around Queenstown. Climbers modelled all sorts of gear in front of a mountain range. There were kayakers being thrown around in some impressive white water and even a shot of a tandem bungee jump off a bridge over a gorge.

And that could be the key, Fizz decided.

Was part of the barrier Cooper had between himself and the future he deserved tied in with his over-zealous attention to the safety of others? What if she could show him that it was possible to take a risk, purely for the enjoyment of the adrenaline rush? That the world didn't necessarily fall apart. Even if it didn't totally break through that barrier, it would be a good start, wouldn't it? A physical push that could lead to emotional freedom?

Fizz handed over her credit card and turned to grin at Cooper as he stood waiting for her.

'I can't wait to get to use this clothing,' she told him. 'Queenstown, here we come...'

CHAPTER NINE

LIFE JUST DIDN'T get much better than this.

Fizz had the window seat on the plane that was coming in to land at Queenstown's airport so Cooper had to lean close enough to catch the scent of her skin in order to soak in the view of impressively craggy mountain ranges against an endless blue sky reflected in the huge lake beneath.

For a moment, the sight of mountains did what they always did and caught at Cooper's heart with a memory of his brother, but it wasn't a painful reminder. If anything, the remembered flash of excitement in his twin's eyes that had always lit up with the challenge of a steep track or some rocks to scramble over was simply added to his own anticipation of this weekend's training course.

There were interesting subjects to be covered and Cooper was keen to learn new skills in tracking and being able to recognise the smallest clues or signs that someone had gone through an area. The refresher course in search methods and the psychological aspects of the kinds of behaviour that lost people could demonstrate would be useful and the day outdoors in the back country was even more exciting. They would be practising bushcraft and survival skills like river crossing and would even create and then sleep in an emergency shelter.

It was exactly the kind of weekend that Cooper loved more than any other because it combined his thirst for new knowledge and challenges with his passion for being prepared to help anybody in any situation. He would happily take on the role of in-house training for other members of the team at the Aratika Rescue Base and he was hoping to find an active search and rescue team in the Wellington area so he could make himself available to help whenever possible.

Best of all, he was in the company of a person who shared his passion. Maybe Fizz had different reasons for being here and her desire to learn more about search and rescue was largely due to her love of adrenaline-producing situations, but right now the motivation was irrelevant. Cooper was already addicted to being in the company of this woman who could make him feel so alive, and they were going to be sharing something new and exhilarating in the next couple of days that could only bring them closer.

If circumstances conspired to bring Fizz a little closer, would she realise how perfect they were for each other and change her mind about allowing a true relationship into her life?

Fall in love with him, even?

She certainly seemed to be delighted to be with him and it had been her idea to come south a day early when they discovered that their rosters made it possible.

'We'll go and have a bit of fun,' she'd suggested.

'I'll find an adrenaline rush for you that you won't be able to resist.'

Fizz almost had her forehead pressed against the window as she stared down at the extraordinary landscape beneath the plane. A bump of turbulence distracted her and she turned to catch Cooper's gaze for a heartbeat. Instantly, her face came alive with her smile and the sparkle in her eyes.

'Gorgeous, yes?'

'Oh, yeah...' But Cooper kept watching Fizz as she turned back to make the most of the view as the plane descended.

He was thinking back to their conversation about this high country and mountain rescue training weekend, so many weeks ago, when they'd gone out to dinner the night Harrison had broken his arm. When he'd told her that it might be a good thing for her to have to learn a few safety rules. When she had told him that a bit of adventure tourism might be good for *him*.

Would it impress her if he did embrace some adventure? Prove that he wasn't overly safety-conscious because he disapproved of chasing that adrenaline rush? Maybe it would make a real difference to show Fizz that he really did understand the forces that were so much a part of her life and that he was prepared to share them. That this didn't have to be simply a weekend of adventure together. It could, in fact, be the beginning of a lifetime of adventures.

Cooper sat back in his seat and tightened his seat belt as the turbulence increased. When Fizz caught his hand to hold it he wondered if the rough air was bothering her but then she gave his hand a squeeze and he caught her grin. She was loving every moment of this ride, probably more so because of the turbulence.

He was going to make the most of every moment as well, Cooper decided, and he was definitely up for whatever kind of fun Fizz was planning to challenge him with for the rest of the day. Zip-lining, skydiving, white-water rafting—he wasn't going to point out any dangers in these extreme forms of pleasure seeking. He also wasn't going to think about the possibility of their connection ending any time soon because it was no longer fun for Fizz.

Cooper was going to make sure she'd never had so much fun in her life.

The wall of pamphlets in the tourism office made the choice overwhelming.

They'd picked up a rental car, left their bags at their motel near the location of the course venue and then they'd come straight into town so that they could squeeze as much as possible into this day of freedom before the course started tomorrow, and Fizz was on a mission.

She was going to push Cooper Sinclair's boundaries—enough to put him out of his comfort zone. Enough to challenge his preference to keep people physically safe. And to keep himself emotionally safe.

'So…what's it going to be? The famous jet boat experience in the gorge? Skipper's canyon? Skydiving or bungee jumping?'

'This cruise on the *TSS Earnslaw* looks great.' There was a twinkle in Cooper's eyes that told her he was teasing her. 'What a beautiful old ship.'

'You can do a cruise on Lake Wakatipu when you're old and grey and want to eat cake with a fork.'

Fizz looked away to reach for a different brochure. Or was it that she didn't want to reveal the odd frisson that that teasing glance had given her? A delicious ripple of sensation that had nothing to do with how physically attractive this guy was, or how much she respected his intelligence, for that matter. It was simply about how much she enjoyed his company. How good it felt to be around him.

'How about mountain biking?' she suggested. 'Look…you can take the gondola up to the top of that peak and then ride all these trails down.'

'I'll bet the view is amazing from that restaurant at the top of the gondola. Maybe we could aim to go there for dinner.'

'Okay…but only if we go and do something really exciting first. Choose something, Coop.'

'I choose that.'

Fizz followed the direction of his gaze to the large poster on the wall. Climbers on a sheer cliff face with a waterfall right beside them and the view of the valley beyond that made it clear they were a very long way up the side of a mountain.

'I'm not that experienced at climbing.'

'You don't have to be.' A young man came out from behind the desk. 'Even children can do the easier runs. You're clipped in at all times. Every hold is a rung that's secured into the rock. Every bridge has cables so you're never in danger of falling. I've done it myself and…' He blew out a breath. 'It's wild, man…you really should do it.'

Cooper was grinning at her. 'What do you reckon? Want to give it a go?'

'Do *you* want to give it a go?' It might be safe but Fizz was sure that it would be an adrenaline-producing activity. Probably downright terrifying at times. And how would Cooper feel about rock climbing on a mountain, anyway? Wouldn't that bring back potentially overwhelming memories of the way his brother had died?

But he was holding her gaze now and there was something in it that Fizz didn't recognise. Something that was nothing like as light as his usual glint of mischief but not as heavy or serious as when they were working together in some emergency situation, either. It looked almost like a question. Or a promise?

'I'll give anything a go,' he said. 'If it's something you want to do.'

'Really?' Fizz gave up trying to process what seemed different about that gaze.

This was perfect—exactly what she'd been hoping to encourage Cooper to do, and if it did push him a bit further than she had intended by being an activity with powerful associations with his past, maybe that was even better. She could help him through it. Show him that there were no barriers that could prevent him having the kind of future he deserved, and that he would have a friend for life who would always encourage him to chase any dreams.

She turned to the young man beside them. 'Sign us up.' She smiled. 'Can we do it this afternoon?'

What had he done?

Cooper stared at the countryside in front of him.

He was sitting in the front passenger seat of a four-wheel-drive vehicle. Fizz was in the back alongside a pile of gear and their guide was driving them closer and closer to what should have been simply a picture-postcard scene of a waterfall cascading down a ravine between rocky cliffs.

He could have chosen anything that would have been enough of an adrenaline rush to impress Fizz with his risk taking and would have taken no time at all—like a jet boat ride or a rafting trip through a stretch of churning white water, perhaps. Or a bungee jump that would have been over in a matter of seconds. But no…he'd picked an adventure that was going to take hours and present challenge after challenge that would probably be emotional as much as physical.

They were going to climb right up to the top of this spectacular waterfall, climbing sheer cliffs, crossing the ravine over multiple bridges and even going behind the rushing water at some point. Mountain climbing. Something Cooper hadn't been remotely tempted to try since his brother's death.

What *had* he been thinking?

He glanced over his shoulder, wondering if Fizz was having any second thoughts about his choice of activity, but she was staring ahead through the windscreen and the expression on her face was anything but doubtful. She had that glow, like she'd had when they'd been bouncing through that turbulence, coming in to land earlier today. Like she'd had that first day he'd met her. When she'd emerged from underwater where she'd been trying to free the woman trapped in that car and she'd been braiding her hair to get it under control, and she'd looked as if putting herself into danger to save someone else had been so exciting she'd do it all over again in a heartbeat.

And he'd found something inspirational in that kind of passion. Because…because she'd reminded him of Connor, hadn't she? The person he had loved the most in all the world. The more reckless twin who had always thrown himself at life with such determination and had got so much joy out of his exploits. The one who'd always pushed Cooper to be the best—and bravest—version of himself that he could be.

Maybe the choice of this challenge had been subconscious. Confused, perhaps, because he would be doing it with the person who had so quickly become what he'd never thought he'd have in his life again—someone he loved so much that their safety and happiness seemed more important than his own.

The beat of fear that Cooper was aware of as he turned back to see that the mountain was even closer didn't have anything to do with the challenge they were about to face. It was more about how he would cope if he lost Fizz. Or if he could never tell her how he really felt about her—that she was the one person he wanted to be with for the rest of his life. And, even if he didn't say anything out loud, was it possible to feel like this about someone and not let it show?

There was no time to think about anything other than what lay immediately ahead of them when the jeep stopped a few minutes later. There was gear to put on, including a helmet, gloves and a nappy type of harness that had two lengths of synthetic rope attached with heavy-duty carabiners on the ends.

'You'll be attached at all times,' their guide told them. 'You'll only unclip and move one line at a time.

We'll go and do a bit of training on a low set of rungs and cables. You're both good with heights, yeah?'

'No problem for me,' Fizz assured him. 'And my friend, Cooper, here dangles out of helicopters often enough so I'm sure it'll be a walk in the park for him.'

She smiled up at Cooper but he was finding it difficult to smile back.

He was only her 'friend'?

An echo of that beat of fear returned. How hard would it be to spend time with this woman if this stopped being fun for Fizz and it was over? Would she have any regrets?

Probably not. There was another echo in the back of his mind now. Fizz's voice saying something about living for the moment and enjoying something while it lasted. Moving on with no regrets when it stopped being fun.

Cooper saw the flash of concern in Fizz's dark eyes. She stood on tiptoe to plant a swift kiss on his lips.

'Don't worry,' she murmured. 'It'll be as safe as houses. Just like climbing a ladder.'

Finally, Cooper could find his smile. Fizz thought he was simply concerned about how safe this was going to be. Maybe it *was* going to be possible to hide how he felt about her and keep things going a whole lot longer.

With the faint tingle of the touch of her lips still on his own, Cooper set off, lengthening his stride enough to catch up with Fizz and walk by her side.

This adventurous afternoon had been an inspired choice for something exciting to do in a very beautiful place.

Fizz was having the time of her life. This might be a very safe thing to do but it didn't actually feel like that when you were halfway up a completely sheer cliff or crossing a bridge that was no more than a single cable to put your feet on, with extra cables for both hands and an overhead one that your carabiner clipped onto. With a drop of hundreds of feet below and the rush of water almost close enough to touch, the sense of doing something intrepid and brave was...well, it was just perfect.

It wasn't the sort of thing that she would have expected safety-conscious Cooper Sinclair to be enjoying. It wasn't that he didn't do dangerous things in his job but he did them to help others, not purely for the personal enjoyment of an adrenaline rush.

He was doing this for her, wasn't he? Because he knew how much of a thrill she got from successfully challenging herself like this. Because he wanted to impress her, perhaps?

Not that he needed to. He was impressive enough just the way he was, even with that annoying overprotective edge that he had. Cooper was a clever, very skilled, warm and caring person. He was mischievous enough to be great fun to be with and he was certainly the best lover Fizz had ever had.

Right now, he had taken his first step onto the cable bridge and, with his extra height and weight, he was swaying a lot more than Fizz had. She saw him try to control the sway by going still and she saw the deep breath he took when he turned from looking sideways, at the panoramic view of green flat land with a lake and snow-capped mountains in the distance, to the drop beneath that slim cable he was trying to stand on.

'You're doing great,' their guide encouraged him. 'Just take it slowly. One step at a time.'

Cooper nodded and then looked directly ahead, to where Fizz had reached the other side of the ravine and was waiting for him before tackling the next upward ladder of rungs.

Steadier now, Cooper took a careful step forward. And then another. He was holding Fizz's gaze and she could feel her smile widen into a grin. She was proud of him, she realised. He was really stepping out of his comfort zone here and he was doing it with style. That he was probably doing it only because she was with him made her feel curiously protective. She wanted him to enjoy this. To want to push his boundaries. To believe that he could do anything and be anything he wanted to be in life.

That he could have everything he deserved.

Like a family who would adore him.

Not that there was any hurry for him to go and find the person he could create that family with. Fizz didn't want this adventure to end any time soon. Being with Cooper was more than fun. It was kind of like that space you got when you'd done something incredibly exciting and then arrived at safety. The time when adrenaline levels had lowered enough to make you feel tired but happy.

When you got the heightened feeling of how great it was to be alive but you only appreciated it that much because there'd been a chance that you might not be alive now. It was about being totally in the moment and taking a deep breath to revel in it but also knowing that it would be possible to experience that thrill again sometime soon. A feeling of being safe but with no limits on what could happen next. Safety laced with pure excitement.

How much more fun was it going to be sharing her spare time with Cooper if they could both go out and pursue adventure together? She could take him on four-wheel-drive outings that were a lot less tame than Ocean Beach had been. Or maybe they could both get involved with a mountain rescue team after the course this weekend and get deployed on missions that would take them into countryside like this. Challenges that might not have a guide and so many points of safety to clip onto.

Fizz would still feel safe. Who wouldn't with someone like Cooper watching out for you? She could feel the solid shape of his body as it came closer to her end of this bridge. Solid and warm and totally trustworthy.

Oh, yeah…she didn't want times like this to end anytime soon.

They rode the gondola—advertised as being the steepest cable car lift in the southern hemisphere—up to the restaurant perched high above Queenstown. It was the perfect place to watch daylight fade over the stunning view of the lakeside town with its backdrop of the dramatic skyline of the Remarkables mountain range. The twinkle of lights coming on bit by bit sprinkled a note of celebration to their evening. They were drinking a local, Central Otago wine that was delicious and the food they were sharing was equally good.

'I think this has been one of the best days of my life,' Fizz sighed happily. 'How amazing was that climb?'

'It was extraordinary,' Cooper agreed. 'I knew it

was safe enough but I have to admit it had its moments.'

'I know… Like when we were halfway up that longest set of rungs on that totally smooth rock face. I got a bit of vertigo when I looked down.'

'And I thought of what might happen if one of the rungs came loose from the rock.'

'It would have been okay. We were clipped onto the cable as well.'

'And those bridges. The plank was hard enough but tightrope walking on that single cable felt impossible.'

'But you did it.' The slow way that the corners of Fizz's mouth were curling was the most gorgeous smile Cooper had ever seen. 'I'm so proud of you, Coop.'

'You know what?' Cooper smiled back at her. 'I think I'm quite proud of me, too. I learned something about myself today—thanks to you. And I would never have thought of doing something like that by myself.'

Fizz's eyes darkened with empathy as her smile faded. 'Because of Connor?'

Cooper's breath caught in his chest. Or maybe it was something else catching his heart. The feeling that Fizz saw parts of him that nobody else ever would? That she cared about the things in his life that had shaped who he was today and who he would be in the future? That she understood, so well, what it was like to lose someone so important in your life?

He found himself nodding slowly. 'I was thinking about him a lot. He would have loved to do that climb *so* much. He was an adrenaline junkie, I guess. Like you.' But Cooper was smiling, to let Fizz know that wasn't a criticism. 'That look on your face when you let go in the middle of that bridge and you were just sitting in space with your weight in your harness and your arms out wide and you had that…glow… It's what I remember about Connor whenever he was doing something that excited him. It always made me happy to see *him* so happy. So…alive… If only I'd…'

Fizz reached out to touch Cooper's hand. 'Don't do that,' she said softly. 'No more "if onlys". It wasn't your fault. Maybe he wouldn't have even listened to you if you'd tried stopping him because he was chasing that feeling of being so alive that nothing else mattered in that moment.'

'I kind of get that now. But I still feel that I should have stopped him. I knew it wasn't safe enough. It had been raining. The rocks were slippery.'

'It was an accident,' Fizz said. 'They happen. And sometimes you can be too careful and you'll miss out on a lot of good stuff that way. The only way you could ever make yourself totally safe would be to shut yourself inside an empty room and never do anything, and what kind of life would that be?' Her smile was wry. 'You could still get sick, too. Or fall over and break your neck. Things happen, Coop. You lose people. You lose people that you love very much, but if you let that hold you back, you may as well be shut in that room, don't you think?'

Was she talking about herself as well as him? Was this, in fact, an invitation to a different kind of future? The vision of a future Cooper wanted more than anything he'd ever dreamed of was filling his head. And his heart. A future with this woman he was loving more with every day that passed. A future that didn't have a 'use-by' date for when the 'fun' stopped. A real relationship? After those passionate words Fizz had just uttered, the hope surrounding that dream was so real he was convinced that they were on the same page. Thinking the same thing. That they were both prepared to take the risk of truly loving someone and committing to spending their lives together.

'I love *you* very much, Felicity Wilson,' he said quietly. He turned his hand that she was still touching so that he could catch hold of hers. 'And I never, ever want to lose you. To be honest, I'm starting to have trouble imagining my future without you.'

Time seemed to stop in that instant. He could almost see the moment his words reached her brain and she understood what he was saying. Precisely the same moment that the colour began to leach from her face.

'*No...*' The sound was no more than a whisper.

He could feel her hand dragging itself free of his.

'Excuse me.' Fizz pushed her chair back and got to her feet. 'I need to…um…go to the loo.'

Really? Cooper wondered. Or was it that she needed time to find the words she needed to let him know that she didn't feel the same way?

He could see the way her chin tilted before she shook her head sadly. 'Oh, Coop,' she said quietly. 'Why did you have to go and say something like that?'

'Because it's true.' Cooper wasn't going to apologise. He felt sick at having clearly misjudged the moment so badly but he couldn't feel sorry for being honest. He didn't want to have to hide how he felt. It was far too big to be able to hide, anyway. 'And it's not something that's going to change.'

For a long, long moment, Fizz stood there staring at him. So long that Cooper actually felt a beat of that hope again. That she might tell him that she felt the same way. That, maybe, there was hope that she could get past the trauma of losing the man she had planned to spend the rest of her life with and that she was ready to try again.

It was hard to tell in the candlelight around their table but there was a glint in her eyes that could be due to unshed tears. Or possibly anger.

'You've ruined everything,' Fizz murmured.

Cooper still couldn't be certain whether she was angry or sad and he didn't get any more time to wonder because Fizz had turned on her heel and was leaving the restaurant so quickly she was virtually running away from him.

Running out of his life…

CHAPTER TEN

THERE WAS NOWHERE actually to run to but Fizz couldn't go and shut herself away in a bathroom.

They were on the top of a small mountain and, as far as Fizz knew, the only way down was in the gondola or via the tracks in the mountain bike park, which was undoubtedly closed after dark. She kept going, anyway. Past the bathrooms and the entrance to the restaurant. Past the area where you waited for a gondola cabin to arrive.

'Oi!' The crew member in charge of getting people safely in and out of the gondolas called after her. 'Where are you going, love? The next stargazing tour doesn't start for thirty minutes.'

'Just need a bit of fresh air,' she called back. And freedom, she thought. She was feeling trapped. By walls. By words. By the thought that she might risk everything by trusting a future that couldn't be trusted.

'Well, don't go far,' the man warned. 'It's dark out there. Easy to get lost.'

Fizz nodded but kept going. She simply had to get away.

Cooper loved her?

He couldn't see a future without her? It had prob-

ably only been a matter of minutes before he'd want
to start talking about a wedding. A honeymoon. Having a family and planning how they could fit their
careers around shared parenting. Making promises
about 'for ever'.

How had she not seen that coming?

Fizz had always sensed when one of her male
friendships was getting out of control and someone
wanted far more than she was prepared to offer them.
It hadn't always been easy but each time she'd managed to escape without hurting anyone too much in
the process.

But she hadn't seen it coming with Cooper. Why
not? Because she'd believed that he was held back by
the same barriers she was. The kind of barriers that
were built, brick by painful brick, from the pain of
losing someone so special that life could never be the
same. Losing hope that the future would be the way
you assumed it would be. The way you wanted it to be.

Fizz knew the answer to that question, of course. It
had been so blindingly obvious in that moment when
she'd turned her back on Cooper and tried to get as
far away from him as she possibly could. She'd been
drawn to him from the moment she'd met him. She
admired every quality he had. She believed that he
deserved the best that life could offer and she'd believed that she could help him achieve that by being
his friend. By pushing him to overcome any barriers
that might be holding him back.

Well, that had just backfired in a fairly spectacular
fashion, hadn't it?

Cooper *had* overcome his barriers. And by doing
so, he'd given Fizz a clear glimpse into what had been

sneaking up on her. She'd come *so* close to falling into that moment when he'd been holding her gaze and telling her that he loved her. So close to telling him that she felt the same way. To making promises and those plans for a shared future.

She had recognised what Cooper Sinclair was searching for because...because it was what she was searching for herself. She'd just been too blind to see it.

She wanted all the good things life could offer to Cooper because...because she loved him. She loved everything about him. She had wanted to keep this friendship with benefits going as long as possible, not just because she enjoyed his company so much but because she felt the same way Cooper did. She was having trouble imagining her own future without him as a part of it.

This was the worst thing that could have happened. She was in love with Cooper and she wanted that future, too—possibly more than he thought he did. She wanted to see him every day for the rest of her life. To hear his voice. To feel the touch of his hands or his lips.

She wanted his babies...

Fizz was in the position she'd sworn never to be in ever again. With dreams and hopes for a future. And it felt like a huge, emotional, wrecking ball was swinging through the air directly at her. Waiting to show her how destructive it could be when those hopes and dreams were wiped out in an instant.

She couldn't go there again.

She wouldn't survive a second time.

Fizz had gone past a helipad now, and signs showing her the direction to take if she was here for a luge ride or a tandem paraglide. Good grief...that was kind of ironic, wasn't it? As if she needed reminding that clearly of how easily dreams could be snuffed out.

She turned away from the signs, away from the defined pathway, heading for the edge of the pine forest. Maybe being amongst trees with no sign of human habitation for a few minutes would ground her again and this feeling of panic would subside. That wrecking ball would not be able to get close enough to do any damage at all. Trees were huge and solid and safe.

Like Cooper was?

Oh…help. Half-blinded by tears, Fizz set off into the forest. There was a warning bell sounding somewhere in the back of her head with tones of getting lost, of tripping over a tree root and breaking her ankle, but there was no way she could stop just yet.

She'd tried to persuade Cooper to stop feeling guilty over his brother's death by telling him that he might not have been able to stop Connor from having that accident because his brother had been living so much in the moment he wouldn't have listened. That's what Fizz felt like right now. Even if Cooper was somewhere behind her and yelling at her to stop, she wouldn't be able to. It wasn't the thrill of an adrenaline rush that was pushing her forward, though. It was fear.

Fear of putting her arms out to hold tight to what had become so incredibly important to her only to have it snatched away again.

Cooper…

A sob escaped her lips at the same moment that Fizz felt the ground beneath her feet begin to slide away. She reached out to catch a tree branch but it snapped and slipped through her hands as her speed increased. And then she lost her balance and hit the ground hard. She could feel herself rolling now and protruding rocks were hammering at her body, which was scary but not nearly as terrifying as when that pain suddenly stopped and Fizz knew she was falling over the edge of a cliff.

She was going to die, she realised in that moment, but the sound that came from her lips wasn't a scream of terror.

It was simply a name.

'Cooper...'

He sat there for several minutes.

Well, he couldn't have chased Fizz into the ladies' toilets, could he, however much he might have wanted to. And he trusted that was where she'd needed to go because Fizz wasn't someone who would simply run away from something. She was the bravest person he'd ever met.

It was clear that he'd said too much, too soon. That he'd ruined everything. So, for a few minutes, Cooper sat there and felt a bit sorry for himself. Sad that a future he'd truly believed would be all he could ever hope for in his life was not going to be possible. Sorry for Fizz, as well, because she needed more in her life than a brilliant career and the excitement of chasing adrenaline rushes.

Everybody needed to be loved and he could do that. He could love her with all his heart and soul for every day they were lucky enough to have together.

The way she'd been looking at him, on more than one occasion today, caught in his mind. Sharing the excitement of flying into Queenstown this morning and looking as if he was the only person she wanted to be here with. When he'd been walking towards her on that single cable tightrope, swinging over a scarily high drop to the rocks below, and she'd looked… well, *proud* of him—as if his achievements were just as important to her as her own.

And, just minutes ago, when her empathy for the loss of his brother had been written all over her face and the touch of her hand on his had given them a link that had seemed so much more than merely physical. It had felt as if their hearts were connected. Their souls, even. It had been enough to make Cooper believe that she was thinking that they could both escape from a space where a real relationship was not going to happen. That they could both get out of that safe but confined space—that empty room she'd been talking about that was no kind of living—because surely being too careful applied to emotional safety as much as anything physical.

The more Cooper thought about it, the more he could remember what he'd seen in Fizz's eyes and he could add that into so many moments when they'd been together in these last weeks and wrap those moments inside the cloak of the extraordinary physical connection they'd found in their lovemaking.

He got to his feet.

He wasn't going to push Fizz into doing anything she didn't feel comfortable doing but he wasn't going to let this die by letting her run away without at least talking about it. At some level, he really didn't believe that she wanted that, either.

And…she'd been in the toilets for rather a long time, hadn't she? Cooper went to take care of the bill. They would have to both return to the motel room where they'd left their bags, so that would provide an opportunity to talk if nothing else.

A woman with a small child was coming out of the ladies' toilets when Cooper left the restaurant.

'Is there anyone else in there?' he asked.

'Don't think so,' the woman replied. 'No, I'm sure there wasn't.'

Cooper went further. He got to the gondola station. 'Did a woman take the gondola back down?' he asked. 'About ten to fifteen minutes ago?'

The man shook his head. 'I saw her, though,' he said. 'She said she needed a bit of fresh air. I thought she might be waiting for the next stargazing tour.'

'Which way did she go?'

The man shrugged. 'She won't have gone far, mate. It's too dark on the tracks now. You'll find her.' His sympathetic glance suggested that he thought they were an arguing couple that needed to make up. 'Good luck,' he added, before shaking his head. 'Women, huh? Can't live with them, can't live without them…'

Taking the gondola down these steep slopes would be the only safe way to descend at night but Cooper knew all too well that Fizz wouldn't hesitate to take a less safe option. She would probably prefer it, in fact.

He wandered the areas that were well lit, ignored barriers that carried warnings of being out of bounds and used a flashlight app on his phone when he followed a smaller track and found himself in the darkness of a fairly dense pine forest. It would have been useful to have already done the course they were intending to do tomorrow, he thought. He could do with some extra knowledge of how to tell if someone had walked along these tracks recently. How long ago had that branch been broken, for example, and had it been done by a human or an animal? Was that a fresh footprint or a scuff from a mountain bike tyre? He tried sending a text message and calling Fizz but received no reply.

He should go back, he realised a short time later. He could ask for help in searching for Fizz. But what if she'd simply walked down one of the main tracks and was now safely in their motel room? Sending out a search party that could actually involve some of the personnel they might meet in their course this weekend could end up being a source of acute embarrassment. It would also increase the distance appearing between himself and Fizz by shining a spotlight on how differently they approached life, and that was the exact opposite of what he'd hoped to achieve by joining her in some adrenaline-producing activities today.

Nobody would launch a search and rescue mission at this time of night, anyway. They would wait for first light so that they could see what they were doing and keep everybody in the search team as safe as possible. And perhaps Fizz hadn't headed back to the motel. She could have circled back to the restaurant after giving herself a bit of breathing space and be in there now, wondering where on earth *he'd* got to.

Cooper turned back, looking for the gleam of light through the trees to show him the direction he needed to take.

And that was when he saw it. The pale gleam of a small branch where it had been snapped.

It had to be fresh. Part of the branch was hanging on by a thread of bark that would snap at any moment due to the weight that was gradually tearing it from the rest of the branch. Cooper approached cautiously, using his torch to scour the surrounding ground. He could see that the ground was starting to slope steeply even before he got near the broken branch. And he could see the marks where someone had slipped and where those marks suddenly vanished.

All Cooper's training was telling him exactly what he should be doing right now. Marking his trail as he went to call for professional help. People who had the kind of gear that would make navigating this landscape so much safer. Headlamps, for example. And ropes. Abseiling gear. A stretcher in case it was needed for someone that was badly injured...

That did it. Cooper couldn't turn around. Not when that injured person could be the woman he loved.

Very carefully and slowly, he edged down the steep slope towards the drop, using tree branches and rocks for support. He lay down then, to peer over the edge, but he couldn't see anything but more rocks and vegetation.

'Fizz?' His call was tentative. 'Are you there?'

He listened carefully but could hear nothing apart from the sound of the gondola mechanism as its cars moved along the cable not far away. The hum and clicks slowed and then got quieter and it was in that moment that Cooper heard something that sounded very much like a groan.

'Fizz?' He scrambled a bit further down the slope, hoping that the branch he was using for support was not going to snap under his weight when he felt his feet slipping at one point.

'Cooper?' The call was faint. 'Is that *you*?'

'Yes... Where the hell are you?' Stupid question, he realised as soon as the words left his lips. How on earth would she know? 'Keep talking,' he called. 'I'll find you.'

'I'm sorry...' The words floated through the darkness. 'It was a stupid thing to do...'

'That doesn't matter right now...' Cooper pushed sideways towards the sound of her voice but found a barrier—a deep fissure between two rocks. 'Are you hurt?'

'I'm not sure. I slid over a few rocks on the way so I'm sure I'll have some bruises. There were some bushes that broke the fall quite a bit and I might have bumped my head when I landed. Scratched it, anyway.'

He was much closer now. The place where Fizz had landed was right behind the rock on the other side of this fissure, where there appeared to be a ledge. As Cooper shone his torch on the rocks to try and assess whether it was possible to get across the gap, the light caught movement on the other side. A hand appeared on the top of the rock and then he could see Fizz's face as she hauled herself upright. He hair was a wild mess around a face that looked far too pale and she had a streak of blood on her forehead and cheek.

'Don't move,' he told her. 'I'm coming over.'

'No...' Fizz looked dazed but she was staring at the gap in the rocks between them. 'You can't do that. It's far too dangerous.'

'You're hurt.'

'I'm okay. I can wait for help. Coop...don't *do* that...'

It was too late. Cooper had chosen a foothold on this side. All he had to do was make sure he could catch what looked like a suitable handhold on the other side and he would be able to scramble onto the ledge. If he missed—or slipped, of course—it could be disastrous but Cooper felt completely confident. Plus, he didn't give himself time to tap into any familiar safety checklists.

There was a split second as he hung over the gap when Cooper thought his confidence might have been misplaced but he found a boost of strength so that he could push with his feet on one side as he hauled himself up on the other and then there he was, right beside Fizz. Close enough to gather her into his arms.

Except that she pushed him away.

'How could you have done that?' Fizz sounded furious. 'Have you *any* idea how scary that just was for me?' She burst into tears. 'I could have *lost* you…'

Cooper's heart stopped. He'd never seen Fizz cry. Her head injury must be worse than he feared. But then her words sank in. She'd been afraid of losing him? She would only feel like that if she felt the same way about him as he did about her. If she *loved* him?

'It's okay,' he said softly. 'I'm here, babe. I'm not going anywhere if you don't want me to.'

But she was still crying as she shook her head. 'You have no idea how that felt,' she said again. 'I thought you were going to fall. You could have been injured. Or *killed*…'

'I know exactly how it feels.' Cooper found himself smiling wryly as he gathered her into his arms. 'How do you think *I* feel every time *you* do something risky?'

'Really?' The word came out as a hiccup.

'Really.' Cooper was holding Fizz gently. Part of

his brain was trying to assess whether she was in any pain or having trouble breathing from an injury rather than being upset. 'I wouldn't stop you doing those things, though. It's who you are and I love your courage but...you might have to get used to me trying to protect you sometimes or making sure you don't do something stupid—like running off the edge of a small cliff like this one. Now, let me check you out and then I'm going to call for some help to get us out of here.'

'Not yet... I don't think I'm hurt much. A few bumps and bruises maybe. Don't move, Coop... Just hold me, please?'

Cooper shifted enough to give him a more secure position on the ledge and he pressed a kiss to Fizz's head as she snuggled against him.

'I always thought you were a human rock,' she told him. 'I just didn't realise that you were *my* rock.'

Cooper liked that. 'Always,' he murmured against her hair. 'I'll always be your rock.'

'I was running away because I thought it was all ruined.' Fizz lifted her head and Cooper could see her face clearly as moonlight appeared between clouds. 'Because after you said what you did, I realised that I felt the same way...that I couldn't imagine a future without *you* in it. That I...that I...'

Say it, Cooper pleaded silently. *Say that word...*

'That I...*love* you,' Fizz whispered. And then she burst into tears again.

Cooper held her tighter. 'It's actually a good thing,' he told her. 'You'll see.'

But Fizz was shaking her head. 'It means we'll be in a real relationship.'

'I hope so.'

'And that implies a future.'

'It certainly does.'

'Things like getting married and having babies.'

'Well…not straight away but…we can talk about that sort of thing later, babe. We don't have to plan our entire future the moment we find out that we're in love with each other. One step at a time, hey? And the first step is getting us off the side of this mountain and getting you properly checked out. Are you sure nothing is really hurting?'

'My ankle's aching a bit.'

Cooper sighed. 'Knowing you, that probably means you have a compound fracture. Let me see.' He eased her out of his arms. 'No…don't move there. It's too close to the edge of this ledge.'

Fizz froze.

'It's safe here,' Cooper told her. 'You're safe now.'

'You can't always keep me safe, Coop. No one can know what's going to happen in the future.'

'I know.' Cooper was carefully taking her shoe off. 'But it's like watching someone you love do risky things because that's who they are. You have to do what you can to make it as safe as possible and then all you can do is hope that everything *will* be all right. And it usually is.' He cupped her foot in his hand as he examined her ankle, shining his torch on the skin and then starting to palpate the muscles and joint. 'Does that hurt?'

'A bit. Ow, yes…that hurts.'

'There's no bones poking out. I think you might be lucky and it's only a sprain but it'll need an X-ray.'

'Okay…'

Fizz had never been this subdued before. Cooper

looked up, searching her face. 'I'm still worried about that bump you had on your head. Do you know what day it is today?'

Her eyes looked huge in the moonlight. A corner of her mouth twitched. 'It's the first day of the rest of our lives. Together.'

A huff of laughter escaped Cooper. 'Now I'm *really* worried you've got a serious head injury. That's the cheesiest thing I've ever heard you say.' But he straightened up and cupped her chin instead of her foot and then he leaned closer and kissed her lips with a tenderness he could feel coming from his entire body. 'It's also the most beautiful thing I've heard you say,' he told her when he stopped kissing her. 'Particularly that last word.'

'I don't have a head injury,' Fizz said. 'My thinking is crystal clear. That's why I'm still a bit scared.'

'I get that. It *is* scary.' Cooper kissed her again. 'But you know what?'

'What?'

'Somebody said something to me once that sounded quite wise. Something about being too careful and missing out on a lot of good stuff. About how the only way you could make yourself totally safe was shutting yourself in an empty room, and what kind of life would that be?'

Fizz wrinkled her nose as she nodded. 'That person does sound quite wise. It's a good thing you remembered it after all this time.'

But Cooper was being serious. 'I reckon the same goes for taking the risk of losing somebody you love. If you don't take that risk, you're just going to sit around with an empty room in your heart, aren't you? You're going to be hiding in case you get faced with the pain of loss, but if you hide from that, you're also hiding from the flip side of that coin. The joy it can bring to be with someone that you love.'

'I guess…'

'You'd be choosing to be lonely when…when you could be…' Cooper had to swallow a big lump in his throat. 'Happy,' he finally managed. 'Together. I want you to be happy so much, Fizz. I want to be part of that happiness. To help create it.'

'You already are. I love working with you. I love being with you. I love… I just love *you*.'

'Only you had to take a running jump off a cliff to find out?'

Fizz sounded like she was trying to laugh but it turned into a groan.

'Don't do that again, okay?'

'I'll do my best.'

'If you ever get scared again—of anything…' Cooper wrapped his arms around Fizz again. 'Don't try and hide. Run *towards* me, not away from me, okay?'

He could feel Fizz nodding against his chest. Over the top of her head he could see a flicker of movement well above them.

'*Oi!* Is someone down there?'

Fizz jerked her head up. 'It's the man from the gondola station.'

'Yes,' Cooper shouted back. 'We're down here. Stuck on a ledge.'

'Turn your phone on again. Someone saw the light from the gondola when they were on their way up. We can get some help on the way when we know exactly where you are.'

Cooper turned on the torch app again and held his phone up with one hand. He kept his other arm firmly around Fizz.

'Let's get out of here.' He smiled. 'So we can get on with the rest of our lives. Together…'

EPILOGUE

Six months later...

'Don't move...'

'What?' Fizz turned to where Cooper was standing in the doorway. She paused in her action of winding her hair into a knot on the top of her head because something in his expression was giving her a melting sensation deep inside. 'Why not?'

'Because, right now, you look exactly like you did the first time I ever saw you. You were wearing those same jeans and that T-shirt with the knot, and you were putting your hair up to get it out of your way.'

Cooper walked towards her, that look on his face becoming even more tender. His hands were large enough that they went right around her body as he took hold of her waist. Fizz loved that. She would never get tired of the size of this bear of a man she loved so much. Of his combination of both strength and gentleness. When he lifted her off her feet, a bubble of joyous laughter escaped and she released her hair to let it cascade down her back as she wrapped her arms around his neck.

'You looked like a warrior woman standing on that rock.'

'I *am* a warrior woman.' Fizz had to bend her head to kiss Cooper because he was still holding her well off the ground. 'That's why I need to get on with sorting these boxes.'

'We only moved in yesterday. We made the bed. What more do we need?'

'Things to cook with. And eat off.' Fizz kissed him again as she slid down to escape his hold. 'We're supposed to be having a house-warming party with Maggie and Laura and Jack later, remember?'

'Maybe they could bring stuff. Like tacos and beer. That way, we could go back to bed for a bit.'

'Hmm…' Fizz grinned. 'Tempting, but no. This is our house, Coop. Our first house…'

She took a moment to let her gaze roam the main room of this small, old villa, with its honey-coloured wooden floors, pretty tiled fireplace and high ceiling. A glance through the sash windows showed the greenery of a garden that was overgrown enough to give them complete privacy. It was a bit run down but full of character, and both Fizz and Cooper had fallen totally in love with the property the first time they had seen it. High in Wellington's hillside suburbs, they had a view from their veranda of the harbour in all its glory. They could even see helicopters taking off and landing from the Aratika Rescue Base when they weren't on duty there themselves.

'I want this place looking its best when our friends come to see it,' Fizz added. 'Oh, that reminds me… I must call Tom and invite him as well. He wasn't at work in the ED yesterday.'

'Did I tell you I asked Shirley? She's bringing cake for dessert.'

'That's fantastic. Except now we really do need to get things properly tidy or Shirley will start sorting things herself. Is Joe coming?'

'Yes. And Don and Andy. Pretty much everybody from Aratika, apart from the people on shift.'

'What about that new guy—what's his name?'

'You mean Adam—the new HEMS doctor? You're right. It would be a great way to welcome him to the team. I'll try and find his number.' Cooper turned towards the dining table that was covered with boxes and picked up the closest one. 'Where does this one need to go?'

Fizz gave him a look. 'What's in it?'

'Feels heavy enough to be books.' But Cooper laughed as he put the box down again and pulled the flaps open. 'Okay... I guess I'm a bit excited. We've bought a *house*, babe. Together. How good is that?'

'Very good.' Fizz stepped closer to peer into the box. 'That's your training manual from the mountain search and rescue course, isn't it?'

'Yep. You said you wanted to read it, remember? When you couldn't get time off to go back to Queenstown on the next course they offered us.'

'I was too embarrassed to go back to Queenstown. Have you forgotten all those jokes those guys made about being a bit too keen to see how mountain rescue worked?'

'I shouldn't have told them we were due to do the course ourselves the next day. Guess I was just happy you weren't badly hurt.' Cooper was reaching into the box. 'What's this?' He had a much smaller box in his hand and was starting to remove the lid.

'It's nothing,' Fizz said quickly. She tried to take it from Cooper's hands but she was too slow. He was unfolding the small square of newsprint.

'It's the photo that was in the newspaper!' he exclaimed. 'From the rescue on the day we met.'

'Yeah…' Fizz smiled. 'I ripped it out of a paper a few days after that incident so I could keep it and look at you again. I did it so often I got a bit of a crush on you and I was so embarrassed when I did meet you again on base, I pretended I couldn't remember your name very well.'

'I remember.' Cooper nodded. 'I was devastated.'

'Don't think so. It was the same day when you almost kissed me. When you insisted on looking after my thumb.'

'And there I was thinking it was you who'd almost kissed me.'

Fizz grinned as she folded up the newspaper cutting again. 'I'm admitting nothing.'

Cooper had pulled the other object out of the box. 'A shell?'

'Mmm.'

Fizz was a little embarrassed by this. She'd never been particularly sentimental in her life and had nothing more than a few photos to remind her of her time with Hamish, but she hadn't wanted to throw that shell away when she'd found it in a pocket of her flight overalls a while back now. So far back, in fact, it was part of another life. The life before she and Cooper Sinclair had become so much more than a professional team. Or friends who could have fun without being in a 'real' relationship. They were a personal team, now—as close as two people could ever be and equally committed to their future together. A relationship that was as real and meaningful as it was possible to be.

'You were holding it,' she told Cooper. 'That day you told me about Connor. When we were sitting outside Sarah's house and I asked you how you knew so well what to do to help in a situation like that when someone so young was dying.'

Cooper turned the shell over in his hands but he was looking puzzled.

'I think I kept it because it was the day I realised how kind you are. How caring. What a truly special person you are. When I thought how lucky the person who got you for a partner would be, but I didn't ever think it was going to be me.'

'Ah…' Cooper held her gaze. 'Were you right? Does the person who got me for a partner feel lucky? Do you feel lucky now that we're in a real relationship that everyone knows about? That we've not only moved in together but we've bought our very own house?'

Fizz forgot about the huge list of tasks she had in her head to get their home ready for its first party this evening. Nothing mattered other than this man standing in front of her and that look in his eyes that told her he didn't need an answer to that question at all because he trusted her. He trusted that they were perfect partners and he trusted that they would always be together to cope with whatever the future had in store for them.

Best of all, he'd taught her that it was worth having that trust herself. That, without it, she would have been missing out on a joy that had made her world so much bigger and so much brighter that she had never felt so alive. So incredibly happy.

'I *was* right,' she whispered, reaching up to put her arms around Cooper's neck again. To invite him to bend his head and accept the kiss on offer. 'I feel like the luckiest person ever.'

'Me, too,' Cooper murmured as his lips touched hers.

This conversation could well be leading to one they'd had not so long ago when they'd tentatively explored the idea of getting married, but Fizz hadn't quite been ready to take that step into planning their future and instead they'd turned their energy into finding a home for themselves.

Now that they were in their own home, the fear of tackling something that could tap into old fears was receding. Fizz was here, with her human rock. She had never felt so safe or so happy. If Cooper asked her again, she was going to say yes. If he didn't ask her, maybe she'd just ask him. Would he say yes? Could they turn their housewarming party into an engagement party as well?

It was Fizz who broke the kiss. She kept her arms around Cooper's neck, though, and only pulled back far enough to be able to see his eyes clearly. Then she took in a slow, deep breath. Cooper held her gaze. He clearly knew that she wanted to say something and he was waiting for her to say it.

But their eyes were having their own conversation and, in the end, they both spoke at the same time. With the same words.

'Marry me…?'

Their laughter was no more than a soft huff of mingling breath as they closed the gap between them for another kiss. There was just time to say one more word.

'Yes...'

* * * * *

LET'S TALK
Romance

For exclusive extracts, competitions
and special offers, find us online:

f facebook.com/millsandboon

⊙ @millsandboonuk

🐦 @millsandboon

Or get in touch on 0844 844 1351*

For all the latest titles coming soon,
visit millsandboon.co.uk/nextmonth

*Calls cost 7p per minute plus your phone company's price per
minute access charge

Want even more
ROMANCE?

Join our bookclub today!